DOMINION

BY
SIR PATRICK BIJOU

ABOUT THE AUTHOR

Sir Patrick Bijou lives and writes from the United Kingdom and is the author of several books on finance and fiction. He is known for his extraordinary skills in settling and negotiating peace settlements and international law and is a prodigious legal and political adviser. His diverse writing ability has been influenced by many experiences, making him the success he is today.

Sir Patrick has written many books and articles about the liberation of people, highlighting the issues of those whom the literary world of creative writing has not enlightened. His expedition into content writing has made him a remarkably inspired author and professional communicator.

He has written over 40 non-fictional and fictional books spanning different genres.

Finding his Books.

To find out more about Sir Patrick, visit his website.

www.sirpatrickbijou.com
www.bijouebook.com

TABLE OF CONTENTS

PART 1

CHAPTER 1

It had really been a bad day for Alan; his wife had kicked his ass out of the house, literally kicking his ass as he left, slamming the door in his face. Only an hour before that, he received a call that his job had laid him off. The fact that he'd gotten most of the money from the bank account was about the only good thing that had happened so far this day.

Trudging down the street, he'd already tried the few friends he had to see if he could stay with them for a few days; each had no time for him, space, or hell, just laughed at him. Well, so much for those three friends, sighing Alan headed toward the cheap section of town and might as well get a cheap room for a few days. He just hoped he could find another job soon, starving wasn't something he really wanted to try.

Checking in Alan made his way to the room; damn, he was tired, and the bitch had really drained him of energy with this last fight. Laying asleep took him almost as fast as his head hit the pillow, something that didn't happen to him the last few months. Usually, Alan didn't dream, he thought it had something to do with the stress he wasn't sure, this time though, almost as soon as his eyes were closed, the dream started.

He was floating, where he wasn't sure, it was warm, it was peaceful, something Alan wasn't accustomed to; in fact it was too comfortable. Then just as suddenly, he was standing on the ground, well he thought it was ground he wasn't sure it had a yellowish tint to it, like sand, but this felt like he was standing on a sponge.

Wait, Alan thought this is a dream I shouldn't be able to feel and...? What was that god awful smell? Covering his nose as best he could Alan stepped forward, almost sinking into the soft ... ground? Fuck this shit he thought; this should be solid when I walk on it, rising he was now on top of the ground. Huh? What the hell just happened? Walking for a few minutes almost choking, Alan thought the air was so putrid it needed to clear up so he could breathe better, and like before, the air was suddenly clean, clear, and sweet smelling.

Ok, what the hell is going on? A noise drew him to a clump of small purple ... ugh he guessed bushes; on the other side, what could only be describe as a spiked black ball with eyes, was flinging an energy whip like weapon at a group of docile, pink, slug like creatures. The thing was these pink creatures had six legs and almost human like faces. Alan was about to turn and leave when he heard a single word in his mind, help!

The thought had been tinged with pain and suffering of a type Alan couldn't even begin to imagine. Turning back, Alan was starting to get angry, stepping through the bushes,

Alan faced the spiked ball, which had stopped its whipping, you have to imagine Alan was 6' 2", the spike ball was almost as tall and about four feet across. Alan heard it; think at him who are you? It is a crime to interfere in the emperor's business.

Alan could almost feel venom from the thoughts. I know not of who this emperor is, but you won't hurt them anymore, Alan thought.

Ah a Slimtori lover huh? The ball thought, raising the whip it was about to strike, when

Alan he held up his hand, the ball froze then shook, NO! not a Trictatori! I beg your forgiveness lord! I was only following orders! I beseech you not to kill this unworthy soul!

Alan was a little unsettled and didn't move, in a flash the spike ball drew back the whip aiming for Alan.

What happened next was talked about for days among the Slimtori, as the whip traveled toward Alan it suddenly stopped and reversed course striking the spike ball, the screams Alan 'heard' almost brought a smile to his face. The whip repeatedly struck the spiked ball until there were no longer any sounds or thoughts, then the black shell cracked, and an odd purple fluid began to slowly ooze from it.

Alan couldn't feel any remorse about it; he'd given it a chance, strange thing though, he thought only moments before if the ball attacked he hoped that the whip beat the creature to death. The largest of the pink creatures slowly walked over to Alan bowing it thought to him, we wish to thank you great Trictatori, you intervention has saved all our lives he was about to beat us all to death.

Why didn't you fight back? You are many he was, but one it would have been simple for you all to overpower him, uh it Alan thought stumbling over his words.

The pink Slimtori looked at Alan with a strange look, Fight? What is this fight? We know nothing of this, we are story tellers and record keepers, and the emperor is rounding all of my race up to extinguish us.

If you don't fight or know what it is, what harm could you be to him? Alan asked curious now.

As I have said, we are record keepers; centins ago there was a bold seer who foresaw the emperor's defeat by a strange and extremely powerful Trictatori, so powerful that he could exist in two planes at the same time. It was said that though not as powerful in the dream and spirit plane he was still a force too powerful to be defeated by normal means.

I am new here what is a Trictatori? I do not recognize that word. Alan asked feeling a little stupid.

A Trictatori is you one who can manipulate the air, fire, water, make things they need from other things. The large Slimtori said.

Alan thought a moment it sounded like they were talking about the Sorcerers and Wizards of old but ... he wasn't ... he couldn't ... Thinking a moment, he knew that the Slimtori were starving almost on the brink of passing out, waving his arm he thought of a feast for those there, all their favorite food, poof it was there. All the Slimtori bowed low as they went to eat.

Ok, this shit was getting weird, walking to the large Slimtori he asked if there was a safe place they could go to, yes, but it is so far away, I am sure even with this food most of us wouldn't make it, it sadly thought.

I can get you there when you are finished, I will take you there, Alan thought.

You are Trictatori; why would you help lowly creatures like us? It asked, confusion in its thoughts.

It is the way I am, alright? The Slimtori just nodded and went back to eating.

After they had all been transferred, Alan looked around the thick walled building; there was a lot of destruction, waving his hands; the walls were like new, better even, as Alan had strengthened them over a thousand times stronger. Almost all the Slimtori were amazed having never seen a Trictatori this close.

Alan was about to go, he'd felt a tug every hour for some time now and knew he was about to wake up.

Damn this was a sweet dream, just for fun since none of this was really real, he told all the Slimtori that if they needed him again just call him. When they asked what his name was he responded Alan, there was a collective gasp in all the thoughts he heard. Then he heard them all say A-la-n just as he was pulled back then awoke to the phone ringing.

Damn that was a sweet dream! Shit with powers like those he could do so much damn good in the world but not in this world, good shit never happened here. Setting out, he started looking for another job stopping anywhere they might hire him. Sighing he headed back to his room a lot of prospects but nothing solid yet.

Tried beyond belief, Alan hit the shower almost falling asleep in it, laying down again he was out as soon as he hit the pillow. Just like the night before he landed in almost the same spot, the sound of many feet drew his attention that and the sound of several whips again. Not even needing to look, his anger grew, stepping through the bushes again he saw that the visitors were examining the body of the ball creature. The visitors included a few more of the spike ball creatures, a few creatures that looked like a cucumber with hair, ten legs and four eyes, above all these was a two legged, almost rat like creature hairless and whiskerless.

You! Did you see what happened here? One of the cucumbers demanded a scowl on it's almost face.

Alan just stood there his arms crossed; the rat creature glanced his way and immediately flicked her whip at the cucumber creature.

Your Majesty, we cannot allow such... it started.

You will shut your mouth and pay respect to the Trictatori. The rat like leader's thoughts almost seemed like a shout. Suddenly all the creatures were on guard, though many were also shaking.

This useless creature attempted to use his whip on me, a bad mistake. Alan thought with force, looking at all twenty of the guards with the rat creature. He'd missed the walking snake creatures plus more of the pink Slimtori he'd met the day before.

You will speak with respect to the emperor's daughter, you sho... the cucumber creature began to gag and choke then it spilt into four parts its grey body fluids spewing everywhere. All ten of the snake creatures attacked, chanting and spitting, Alan pushed all that they sent back at them, each screaming as it died. The spike balls were the next to die, they tried to roll over Alan who just moved, motioning his hand down upon his other hand all the spike balls were at once flattened, crushed beyond recognition.

Now then, if you are through playing, release the Slimtori NOW! Or the next one I crush will be you, and there is nothing that they can do. Alan told the emperor's daughter what was left of her guards. I suggest that you go home and don't return to this area again, it is under my protection and believe me I won't hesitate to kill ALL that come here! The last Alan said as he made a choking motion with his hand and the Princess was choking, unable to catch her breath. I hope we understand each other.

The Princess threw a dagger like looks at Alan, sucking in air as soon as Alan released her. This is not over you may be powerful but no one can withstand the entire army. Turning his back to her the Princess started to choke again the last of her guards all rushed Alan, waving his hand time slowed as Alan walked up to each, and to the Princess's horror, he split then re split each of her last guards. Walking right up to her, he looked straight into her eyes that was the last warning walking to the Slimtori, he released them then the Princess, remember, Alan thought to her as he whisked the Slimtori away.

The Slimtori were thanking him again, those from before were happy to see old friends they hadn't seen as they said deysims. They were all discussing what had happened most of those here knew different parts of the old seer's story. Alan had started to feel small twinges that were now moving up into small pulls. Damn, it wouldn't be long now. Sighing, Alan made sure they had enough food and space as he had to enlarge the place a little. Alan was starting to walk out not wanting to vanish in front of the pink creatures, frightening them when a young Slimtori came to Alan, I wanted to offer you this gift, for saving our lives and those today, it said as it handed a small box to Alan. There was a huge gasp, then silence, when the box fell through his hand.

It is you! The seer said he would not try to hide but would be hidden, you are here, but you are not! The large Slimtori from the day before thought, ALL the Slimtori bowed to Alan, this didn't go over well, Alan did NOT want to be worshiped.

With that, Alan walked out and almost immediately vanished, awakening in his room again, he was again almost as tired as he'd been when he'd laid down. This fucking dream was wearing him out, rather than go out he laid back down, falling asleep again within seconds. A vision you might say appeared before him.

"Hello Alan," it said funny but she looked familiar, "Yes Alan, I get that a lot or rather I used to before mankind forgot it's magical roots. You have the strongest concentration of magic in you than anyone else on earth."

"What the fuck are you talking about? Damn, these dreams are getting worse and worse," Alan said a little irritated.

"Oh, I am real, but the only way to talk to you is through your dreams, look when you wake up you'll have the little box the Slimtori gave you, open it when you are ready to actually go TO their planet, ok," with that the little fairy, sprite, or whatever the hell she was, kissed his cheek and was gone. The rest of the day Alan slept with no dreams, no interruptions, ten hours later, he awoke to the sun starting to set.

Alan for a moment, was a little disorientated; sitting up he searched the room for anything familiar. Sadly, he realized he was in just a cheap hotel room. Rubbing his eyes, he realized he'd got nothing done that day, shit! Well, he was exhausted, you can't look if you're dead. Sitting up he at first didn't notice the little box that was sitting beside his bed on the night stand. Getting up he went out to get a bite to eat, hoping he didn't run into the bitch of a wife of his that'd really make for a wonderful fucking day. Returning to his room, he sat to watch a little TV when he noticed the little box from his dream sitting on the night stand.

Thinking he tried to remember what the little woman in his dream had said, open when I was ready for what? Damn it! He hated the fact that he couldn't remember, it was bad enough the fucking box was here in the first place.

An hour later after watching the boob tube, it hit Alan that he'd ACTUALLY killed all those creatures. Running to the bathroom, he began to vomit uncontrollably he'd never taken a life before not even a fly and now here he'd killed over thirty or forty beings. Ok, even though they were extremely evil and he HAD given many of them a chance to give up and move on, which they had refused, still it didn't sit right with him. Slapping his face, he called himself a pussy, knowing that they would have killed HIM with no regrets, no remorse a hell of a lot quicker than he had them.

Still sitting in his chair, Alan heard a little voice say, "Hey idiot for one so powerful you sure are forgetful, open it if you are ready ACTUALLY to go to the Slimtori's planet."

Looking around, he didn't see anyone but he swore that was the little woman's voice from his dream. Sighing he wasn't sure he WAS ready to actually go there; the thing was though if he didn't the creatures would be killed when they were found. Reaching for the box he made sure he had all he wanted to take with him, then cracked the box open. Instantly he was back on the planet though he was actually there this time. Well, the odor had improved a lot since he was here last. Looking around, he started to curse; what the hell was up? Why the fuck did he always wind up in THIS spot? Alan was about to think his way to where the Slimtori he'd rescued was when he heard an even larger sound of movement past the bushes.

Wrapping his arms around him he formed an invisible physical shield, then another magical shield. Stepping out he was met by a huge multitude of troops? He guessed you could call them that though they were laughable at best to Alan. There had to be at least two or three hundred black spike balls, one hundred cucumbers things, another two hundred of the snakes, and it looked like they had a new creature that looked like a combination between a walrus, tusks and all, a scorpion and it looked like dragonfly wings, they had at least a hundred of these.

You there Trictatori, you have disrespected the emperor and the royal family give up now and we will kill you quickly, A tall rat creature in the front screamed at Alan.

Somewhat pissed, Alan gave them an ultimatum, I suggest that you give up now before all of you are destroyed, I am far stronger than you think, and I won't hesitate, not any more, Alan thought to the ten rats like creatures in the front.

Each started to laugh that is till Alan snapped his fingers, and the first rat creature fell over dead its neck snapped in two.

At that moment, half of the snake creatures started to chant and spit, Alan calmly sent everything they sent at him back at the front of the army. Within moments all the spike creatures were on fire and dying; this time all two hundred of the snakes started in hmmm Alan thought this ought to be interesting, bouncing everything off before it even got within ten feet, Alan was starting to get pissed again, making a slashing motion half the snakes heads separated from their bodies.

Do we continue this or do you wish to give up? You've lost part of your troops don't sacrifice the rest, Alan thought as forceful as he could. Again, the rat creatures laughed sending the cucumber creatures out, Alan sighed and snapped his fingers again two more of the rat creatures necks snapped as massive panic erupted in their camp. Still the cucumber things attacked, Alan wipe his head and rubbed his hands together watching as all of the advancing cucumber things suddenly dropped all of them boiling in their own juices.

You've lost well over half your troops and three of your generals give up! Alan wished they had a little sense, god he hated warmongers. Snapping his fingers again four of the remaining eight rat creatures keeled over their necks, now broken. The last of the troops weren't too sure now, the last of the snakes were still chanting, the dragonfly creatures took off toward Alan, sighing, he made a scissor motion with his fingers as all of the dragonfly creatures crashed, all but two bursting as they hit the ground. With that the snakes fled, the last four rat creatures advanced upon Alan, well one did; the other three died before they even got within ten feet. Alan felt something familiar about this last one though he wasn't sure.

You fought well Trictatori Alan, better than I thought you would but this battle is between you and I, the last rat creature said as it advanced through all Alan's shields.

Your energy feels human, yes, I see it now you let the power corrupt you, you stayed here in this place. Alan said, startled to find another almost human here.

You might say that, I became trapped here. I lost the crystal to travel home. The Slimtori refused to make another, they said I knew where it was and refused to remember. After a few years, I didn't care that was 5000 of your years ago, then that piss ant seer saw you killing me, as if. The large rat creature said your power won't work on me as mine is the same.

Alan knew different, blasting the sword from the hands of the rat emperor. For an hour and a half, they blasted away at each other, though he'd gotten a few shots through and had actually hit Alan, Alan had done far more damage. Alan's arms were bleeding; there was a gash on his left thigh, a deep cut on his right leg, his right shoulder was also bleeding. The emperor was faring far worse almost every inch of his body had blood coming from cuts.

Alan was tired, as he saw the emperor was, this has to end soon, one mistake and I'll have him Alan thought. Not long after that Alan saw his chance and cut the emperor's throat, the emperor's mouth opened, he saluted and fell over dead. Alan had to move thinking of the Slimtori he'd rescued, he made it half way there, shit he thought I might not make it. Trying again he made it to the outer wall, not sure he could make it around to the front he drew a door and walked in through the wall. The same young Slimtori that gave him the box, caught him as he fell, there was excited talk as the Slimtori all gathered around Alan. Alan thought he heard them discussing how to heal him and a few strange ideas before the world went black.

Alan awoke in his cheap room, when he tried to move, he was extremely soro; what the hell? Holding up both arms, he saw they were covered with cuts and gashes. Strange thing though, was as he watched, they actually healed in front of his eyes, damn he thought, I should have been healed before now. A little voice spoke next to his ear, "you would have but you took a beating in the battle, a little sleep does wonders," the voice drifted to his other ear, "you should be up in no time."

Alan turned his head and caught a translucent outline of the little woman from his dream. "Damn it's about time I was able to see you." Alan said.

"Not yet, but you will one day, now we've got a lot to talk about. When you're healed, how'd you like a job?" the little woman asked.

Alan smiled that sounded like a damn good idea to him.

Alan awoke the next day with a start after the past week it seemed he was starting to lose touch with reality a bit. Looking at the date on his calendar, reality started hitting home even harder; what the hell? According to the calendar almost a whole week had passed. A moment later a knock came from the door of the room he was in, looking out he shook his head oh great, it was that bitch of a manager.

"I know you're in there! I got that receipt you wanted!" she shouted.

Opening the door Alan put on his best face, the rotund, white haired, short older woman stood there with her arms crossed. "Yes maam," Alan told her, "Had a late-night last night so..."

She held her hand up to stop him, "Look I don't care ok? Just pay each week then we got no problems, just remember the rules no drugs, no loud music, and no sneaking in partners for a few days, or you're out."

Shutting the door Alan could only shake his

head, his light brown hair was longer than he remembered it being. Rubbing his eyes to clear his vision better, he also noticed that he was sporting a week's growth of beard; what the hell was going on?

Suddenly a female like voice sounded in his right ear, almost a whisper, "I am sorry Alan I think I healed you far too much here." A light touch at his forehead opened a flood gate of memories.

Suddenly Alan's eyes flew wide, What!? Hadn't it been a dream? "Where are you? I could see your outline last time; now I'm getting nothing."

"As I said," the whispering voice started again, "I am afraid I healed you far too much, it affected your power as well as your memory. I am endeavoring to remedy this."

Alan's head was already hurting like a bitch, after the little voice said that it had healed him too much, and then he'd felt a light touch to his forehead.

"Again, I apologize Alan, I was afraid that the council had me recruit you too soon. As fast as you healed before I got to you, I can now see they weren't wrong." Alan turned his head and stared at where the voice had been, all he saw was a shimmering, like the heat waves you could see on a hot day.

"There, now then down to business. I was sent to recruit you; you are the first in almost 500 years to show that you have the power." The voice said. "I have been..."

"Wait," Alan interrupted her, "Who are you? I'm a little tired of you knowing me but I know nothing of you."

He almost felt a palatable shock then his head

was flooded with tons of information. "Oh shit! AAAA!!" Alan almost screamed as his head began to throb, "You trying to freaking kill me? Christ!" Alan thought the pain would pass, falling on the bed, no dice as the pain increased till his brown eyes rolled back in his head.

Floating in another dream- like-scape, Alan looked at a sprite or pixie that fluttered in front of him.

"So, your name is Hopix, and you are my guide? No, that's not right; you're my watch dog ah!" Alan said, damn, he thought I don't know whether to be insulted or complimented.

"There's no insult intended, as I told you yesterday, we are offering you a job," Hopix said

"I don't understand if this ... council is so powerful, why can't they attend to their mistakes?" Alan asked.

"True, they are a powerful council, but they can't interfere. They can advance any with the power, but the council has no say after they decide they want to use their power. You see they offer the job; you can reject or accept. Reject after the power is instilled and you can do most what you want off earth. Accept and the council asks you to stop other mistakes that have run other worlds and systems to almost ruin." Hopix said taking a breath. "Almost all your needs will be met, though there are a few they can do nothing about, I am sure you know which ones I am talking about."

Alan nodded, it was as always; he worked his ass off and got really nothing he needed in return and THAT he definitely needed.

Hopix eyes grew wide, then she blushed, she had to teach Alan to stop broadcasting his thoughts so strongly.

"I don't mean to hurry you, Alan but the council needs an answer, we have another that needs taking care of he is almost as bad as the last," Hopix said a small shiver running through her body.

"How long before they have to have an answer?" Alan said noticing that Hopix was still shaking badly.

"Soon before the day is finished," she whispered, "Alan, I hope you accept; this case is somewhat personal to me, so I would also owe you much" Alan was back in his room.

Alan noticed that most of the pain was gone; good at least he'd be able to function while he made a decision. Locking up he decided to visit his wife; maybe she'd have a change of heart.

Knocking at the door, she snatched the door open, "What the fuck do you want? I thought you left! After what you said I'm not sure I..."

"After what I said," He shouted, "I think your memory is playing tricks on you. You're the one who kicked ME out, you're the one who said you didn't need, want, or love me. Let us not forget it was YOU that slammed the door, not me. I can see I wasted my time coming here."

A smirked crossed her face, "A waste, yes, that's what I'd call you! A waste of my time all these years. You're a loser that won't amount to anything. I'll have your shit outside in a day or two," With that she slammed the door even harder in his face. Alan could hear her laughing on the other side of it.

Forget it Alan thought I really have nothing here to keep me, not even our children. I'm sure she's already poisoned their minds against me also.

Alan trudged his way back to the motel, lost in his thoughts he didn't notice the man that was trying to follow him. Alan was almost back to the other side of town, when the man caught up to him.

"Hello Alan," The man smiled, a smile that Alan could see was only a feigned attempt to gain his confidence. "We have a proposition for you. You're a hard man to find."

Looking at the man's hand extended to shake, Alan decided to ignore the gesture, "What do you want?" Alan said a smirk on his face. This man was oozing an almost palatable evil.

"As I said, we have a proposition for you. Work for us, and we can grant you everything you want. Your wife would love you unconditionally, and so would your children. We can make sure that everything you want is granted." The man chuckled a little sinister.

Alan stopped, WHAT!? Looking at the man Alan was suddenly angry, angrier than he'd been in a long, long time. Alan didn't even notice that his hands were starting to glow or that the man was slowly backing up.

"For your damn information," Alan shouted, knocking the man off his feet, "I don't want anything to do with that bitch anymore! Second there is nothing that you," here Alan noticed that the man's ears were bleeding, causing him to pause a second. "Nothing you can give me that will make up for the insult you just gave me! Be gone!" The man groaned as Alan reached out to push him away from his self-surprised when his hand went through the man! "What the hell?!" With that, the image of the man exploded and then was gone.

Storming back to his room, Alan lay down and was out almost immediately, Hopix appeared seconds later in his dream.

"I wish I could have warned you about them sooner," she said, "that was an agent of chaos, one of their better ones, he thought he could turn you easily as he had the others.

I am glad he was wrong, so Alan, do you have an answer? The council awaits."

"Yeah, Alan replied, "there's nothing here for me now that I can see, tell them I accept."

"That's good, we've got another assignment for you," came a voice behind him. Alan turned to see a gnome like creature sitting at a table, "You do this one, and I think you'll have a lot more than thanks from the council," the gnome creature said nodding toward Hopix, who was trying to hold back her terror and joy that Alan was taking this assignment to her home planet. "I'll leave you to it," With that he was gone.

"Your home planet? And just when were you going to tell me?" Alan asked.

"I could not 'til you accepted the assignment; I am not allowed to sway your decision about anything before you decide whether or not you would join." Tears fell unashamedly from her eyes. "It was my fault that the human who rules my planet with an iron fist is there. You see I recruited him; I never foresaw the evil he possessed."

Alan's heart was finally starting to soften in regards to Hopix, "Alright, let's go."

Within seconds Alan was standing on a piece of blackened ground, this isn't right he thought. Slowly the ground turned back to its original colors' blues, greens, and oranges, sighing Alan decided he'd have to get used to the fact that not every where would even be close to what earth was. Within minutes the blackened ground was replaced with a myriad of colors as far as he could see, better, he thought.

Suddenly there was a rumbling sound; turning, Alan saw what appeared to be rolling storm clouds. Reaching out, Alan saw it was a cluster of beings like Hopix. Alan brought all his defenses up fully as they swooped in and commenced to dive bomb him; that is 'til the leader of the cluster stopped within a few feet of him.

"You!" she screamed, "so you are here to stop me? HA! As if! I have had centuries to perfect ALL my skills."

Alan reached out, feeling the being was being controlled, making a scissors cutting motion, the little being screamed and then looked around, confused.

"Where am I?" Looking at Alan, her eyes grew large, "Please protect me," she pleaded, Alan pulled her inside of his shield feeling that she was freed from the others influence.

"I suggest that you, prepare for me. You want to act like a bitch? Then I will strike you down like the bitch you are!" The little being at his shoulder's eyes grew even larger.

"But you don't realize who that is," she said, flying

to get behind him, then fell through his shoulder, bowing low she said, "I didn't realize that you were a mazey also, I apologize I await your orders, master."

Alan's mouth hung open, master?! What the hell?! "Yes I have them all trained!' she laughed evilly, "If it's a fight you want then come for me, we'll see who is the strongest to rule this planet."

"I," spit out Alan in disgust, "do not want to rule this planet I am here to free it from you!

"In your damn dreams, lap dog of the council." The woman sent a huge bolt of fire at him, damn he thought is that all they have? Geez! Turning it back he sent it back through the portal it had appeared from. There was the sound of mass panic from the portal, a scream then it closed. All the little beings were suddenly shaking their heads and looking around confused.

"I have to make sure that she can't do this again," Alan told the little, he guessed you call her a woman with wings, translucent wings, rather skinny like the thirty or forty outside his shields, funny their skin was a light green color. Alan had to admit for green women (with wings) they were kind of sexy; shaking his head he cleared his thoughts not good to be thinking like that. Come to think of it Hopix's skin was more of a whitish color, he wondered why.

Looking at the being bowed before, he noticed that the others were also bowing. "Stop that right now," Alan said, "I will not be worshipped, I am not a god," motioning his hand over the one he'd pulled within the confines of his shield, he saw what had been done to them, and the reason for their fear. Alan removed everything he found that the woman had placed there, then did the same to the others.

"I've removed all the orders she placed in your minds, and this," He made another motion like placing a hat on his head, "will never let her control you again."

All of the little women blinked; their thoughts clear and their own for the first time in over two thousand years.

"H ... h ... how is this possible?" The one within his shield asked, "You are mazey, your kind does not grant freedom to slaves like us." Here she bowed her head as tears fell freely from her eyes, just as suddenly her head snapped up, "You aren't here yet you are, you hurt the other mazey as if it were nothing!" She started to back away from him, "You have met one of my kind before!" This last in whispered tones. "We thought it was only a story that was told to the young ones to keep them in line and give them false hope. You really are here to help us not rule us as the previous two did."

Alan was starting to grow uncomfortable, they were all staring at him with huge round eyes.

"I have to return soon, is there anywhere you can hide? I realize that this many of you together will worry her, but I still want to make sure you are safe for now."

The one within his shield nodded, dropping his shield; they all slowly came to the other there, "I am Tropix, and I sensed you wanted to know my name. Look deep into my eyes, and you will see the place I was thinking of."

Alan nodded, and they were there within seconds, deep underground, it appeared there were a few of Hopix's kind here; many looked to be close to death, and there were several screams as many attempted to flee.

Tropix stepped out and told them all what had transpired; though only a few came out, many were too scared to venture any nearer.

Alan had been looking around, his anger growing more by the second, several of the injured children had been abandoned by the others fleeing, a little girl being looked at Alan then groaned, Alan's attention turned to her. He could see all the cruel wounds she had. Waving his hands over her body, others watched in amazement as the girl grew healthier, then suddenly sat up, looking astonished. Flittering her wings, she hugged Alan fiercely, whispering a truly heartfelt thank you in his ear.

All the elders came forward and listened to Tropix as she again explained what had happened on the surface. Many were in shock though one smiled, "I see you've met

CHAPTER 2

"Hopix," he stated, "Yes, I can see you have, the last, I talked to her she said she would never stop looking for the one to free us. It appears as if she may have succeeded."

Alan's look of shock now was all the proof the elders needed. Alan started to heal the worst cases first, though one he wasn't sure of; making a table of food for all of them was another gift they couldn't stop thanking him for.

"I want to save all of the injured, but that one there," Alan pointed to a female decked out in regal clothes lying apart from the others, "I can't seem to do anything for her; she was also too strong for me to enter her thoughts to heal her there."

The elder nodded, looking at the female there, "That is Queen Glimmer, I am afraid that only the freedom of our people will heal her," Sighing, he sadly shook his head, "She took so many injuries trying to save her people, you actually healed those so she has a much better chance, but as long as we live in terror and are enslaved, she may never wake up."

Alan nodded, looking around, and he thought

they needed better protection. Reaching out he slightly enlarged the area, and made better passages to the surface for air; finally, he struggled to increase the already strong shield, damn it! He knew he was stronger than this! Putting everything he had into it he finally had it where he felt it needed to be.

Looking around, he saw that several of the small beings had also added their power to his, smiling, he felt a hard tug. Shit already? The elder advanced and handed a small box to him, which of course, fell through his hand, nodding the next tug yanked him back.

Opening his eyes barely, he saw he was back in his room damn, he was tired; closing his eyes, Hopix was in the dreamscape awaiting him. "Were you successful? She asked her voice almost pleading.

"I haven't destroyed her yet," he replied, "though I did manage to free thirty to forty of your people, I took them to an underground area with some others of your people and healed all those hurt, though I was unable to heal Queen Glimmer completely."

"You saw Queen Glimmer!" Hopix exclaimed, "then there is still hope!"

Alan nodded; damn, it he hadn't felt this tired in a long time. Hopix's face grew concerned when Alan almost faded.

"It appears you over extended yourself, rest I will handle everything till you awake." she said as she bowed, and he faded. This time no dream, no nightmare.

The rest of the day and the next, Hopix kept a vigil over him. She knew that he had a lot more to do, especially now that the woman knew that he had been there and for all she knew was still there on the planet.

Two days later Alan stirred, damn how long had he been out? Looking around he felt Hopix for the first time next to the bed, still only a shimmer he said, "I have to get back there Hopix. I only freed one of the many squads of your people she has under her control."

"Yes Alan, but you had to recharge before you went back, as you were she could have easily killed you. The council has been monitoring the planet, it appears that the increase in the shield also had another side effect. It seems that she sent another squad, as you put it, into the underground area, as soon as they passed through the shield, they were released from her control. As a result, the council says that her power dropped a bit, she's using my people's power to increase her own!" Hopix growled.

Alan nodded it was as he thought, the only problem was that she was also using the people of the planet as her soldiers as well as her slaves.

"Hopix, I need to be up a while; there is no way I will be able to sleep for a bit; please bare with me I know there is urgency. I will free your people but I have to do this my way," Alan said with a sigh, he could see the worry on her face, he'd probably be the same if he had family in trouble like this.

Taking a walk Alan hadn't realized he was that hungry till his stomach let out a loud roar, shit! That was right he hadn't eaten in almost three days. Turning into dinner, he was about to sit when a man pushed his way past Alan grabbing his arm and dragging him outside.

"Hello Alan," the man said, his eyes slightly glazed over, I can see that we seriously under estimated you. I can assure you that this won't happen again!"

"As I told you before, you have nothing I WANT!" Alan shouted, his anger rising, ripping his arm from the other man's grasp. "I want NOTHING to do with you or your kind!" Again Alan didn't notice his hands were glowing a bright red, though the other did and started to back slowly away.

"You can't hurt me while you are on earth, but I can actually kill you!" the other man said, advancing.

"NO!" Shouted Alan as a scream arose from the other man.

Stumbling a moment, the other man said, "You may kill me, but there are far more to take my..." gagging came from the other man as he slumped to the ground.

Kill him? How would I do that, especially if he wasn't on earth? Turning, Alan went back to the diner, shaking his head damn, he needed to eat.

Alan was trudging his way back to his room, shit things were starting to get stranger and stranger. Opening the door, he sat in the chair, thinking about the day.

"Alan," Hopix said next to him, "are you alright? I felt your distress, but it was over before I could lock onto you."

Alan nodded and started to recount what had happened to him at the diner, "the strange thing though. he said I couldn't touch him as long as I was on earth, but he could kill me. I shouted at him, then he screamed, he said I might kill him, but there were many more to take his place, then he strangled and stopped. I felt him leave the body he'd taken over, Hopix, I have no power on earth, so, how is it possible?"

"I am unsure this planet blocks... ," Hopix started.

"We believe we have an answer for that," came a voice behind Alan. "You didn't actually hurt him here, though you have no power on this planet, you do anywhere else. You reached out to protect yourself without realizing it, you are a rare find. If you continue to free worlds, soon, we feel that the balance of light and dark will once again even out. Hopix's planet will effect a bigger shift because of the total amount of magic wielders on it, more than most, also, she can go home to heal herself."

Alan could only nod, then it was gone as suddenly as it started.

"Oh, Hopix, I met an older one of your people in the underground area with Queen Glimmer, he looked at me and knew I had met you," Alan told her.

"Wait," a shocked Hopix said, "an elder very old feeling and looking?" Alan nodded, and Hopix squealed in delight. "Grandfather! He's alive!"

"Yes, he seemed happy that you had finally done what you set out to do. Shall I give him a message when I return?' Alan asked.

"No, I ... yes, just tell him in private, I will be home soon, I feel that you will finally free them from two thousand years of my mistakes." Alan, could feel the regret and remorse flowing from Hopix, like heat waves off a hot oven.

"I should return, I feel I have more to do. I need to weaken her more before I actually fight her." Alan said with a sly smile as an idea started to form.

Lying down, Alan appeared in the same spot, though everything was as it should appear, good she is obviously more worried about me than re-screwing up the world. Reaching out he could feel the free group of Hopix's people den, they were a long way off. He was about to go there, when he felt another group of tiny people heading his way; sighing, he brought up his shields and a few other surprises. Slowly approaching him, he felt her before he actually saw the squad of the tiny people she was controlling.

"So I've finally found you, I thought you were just a lap dog of the council, but you really are here to take the planet from me. I welcome the challenge, too bad it will mean the destruction of all my slaves to accomplish."

A little pissed off, Alan reached out and made a scissors motion above the group in front of him. Once again, he heard the woman scream; then all of the squad were looking at Alan confused, then they were all bowing to him, reaching, and pulling them all within his shield he smiled.

Only a moment later, another squad attacked from below, as Alan thought they would. Sighing he was always surprised how predictive non-military types were, diverting each as they came up, he soon had all of them within a shield next to him.

"Alright, you bitch, that's four of your precious squads you have lost. I know the more you lose the weaker you are, just think soon, you won't have enough to even light your ass on fire!" Alan laughed when he felt her anger erupt, and another portal opened; this time Alan was ready. Reaching in and grabbing the two most powerful beings he felt were feeding the woman's power, he ripped them lose from her, this time though, she didn't only shriek he felt her fade a moment before she reappeared.

"You cock sucking son of a bitch! When I kill you, I'll make it as long and painful as I can; those are mine!" Again she sent (sigh, again) huge fire balls, almost bored Alan sent back at her but stopped when he felt something different. Drawing the two beings to him, he saw that they looked familiar though he couldn't place them at the moment.

Ah! Alan could see what she was doing, not unlike a trick of decoys he was going to try. Waving his hand, the hidden portal opened, the now false one vanishing; struggling to hold the fire balls and the portal open, he felt the woman beginning to panic. Finally, Alan sent the flaming weapons back at her. He'd have to remember that this wasn't a man he was against. A shrill scream sounded from the portal as he snapped it closed. Looking at the second group, he could even more clearly see the strands connecting them to the woman.

A snarl escaped his lips as he violently ripped the strands from the second squad, again pleased when he heard an extremely painful scream near the portal. Looking around, he saw about seventy-five more of the tiny people staring and bowing at him.

The two who'd been leading each group came to him bowing low, "We await your orders, master," each said, a look of absolute terror in their eyes. Alan's face twisted into a mask of rage but calmed when all of the beings before him began to tremble uncontrollably. Realizing his error, Alan quickly waved his hands over all of them. Many looked up amazed, all the bad thoughts, all the terror was gone, but how? He was a mazey the first male mazey they'd ever seen, not issuing orders immediately.

"I have removed all she did to you, your thoughts are your own, and this," again Alan made a putting a hat on motion, this caused most of the women in front of him, eyes to fly wide. "Will free you; she cannot make you do anything against your will again."

Looking at the two unmoving beings next to him, he felt he had to quickly return to the free people. Gathering all the women, he flashed out, a moment later, he was in the underground area, a few screamed when they all appeared, till the elders stepped forward.

"Mazey Alan, I see ... by the great queen! Please, Mazey Alan, we will clear you a path!"

The same elder that had talked to him before said as he shouted moving everyone out of the way.

Not exactly sure, but almost instinctively, Alan moved forward till he was beside the Queen. Looking at each of the beings he saw that they were the queen but slightly different, moving closer he began to work both into her as slowly and gently as he could. A moment later her eyes opened, and she looked at Alan. Motioning him down, she kissed him, mumbled a few words, and sighed, relaxing, and closed her eyes. Alan's eyes were wide, only the elder had heard her faintly whispered words, he too was somewhat surprised though if what the queen had said was true, then he too might be bowing to this man in more than appreciation.

The healers flew to the queen as soon as Alan moved away, their mouths agape in awe and wonder.

Alan turned and saw the wide eyed elder, walking to him Alan whispered, "I take it you heard?" the elder nodded.

"This is not to leave your mind or lips, we will deal with this as soon as I have reunited the rest of the queen. She is weak and will perish at the moment if I do not capture the rest of her mind. Fortunately, the false ruler cannot use her power any more so I must hurry before she realizes it. I'll return soon," Alan said as he walked to the middle of the area and enlarged it again making it almost twice again as large.

Motioning to the elder again, Alan bent to whisper in his ear, Alan told him the message Hopix had given him. The elder's eyes grew large then filled with tears after Alan delivered the message. Alan looked at the elders expecting them to explain, the same little girl ran to hug Alan, he tried to stop her, but she stopped when she found that she couldn't touch him. There were many gasps when they realized just how powerful Alan was and wasn't even there. The little girl backed up and smiled, "I hope you're here soon, it will be good to actually hug you." Alan smiled and nodded before he vanished; opening his eyes, he sighed he was so tired of this on and off again rescue.

Hopix fluttered next to him. This time he could barely see her outline.

"Hopix, I need to rest, I've freed part of the queen but I have to go back now; there's no time. I can't fail, no I WON"T fail," Alan told her as he grabbed the box.

Hopix's eyes were filled with tears, Alan was nowhere as strong as he needed to be, but he was right he had to go now. Hopix started to speak when Alan opened the box and ... huh? They were both on her home planet! NO! Alan looked over at her and made a strange motion towards her; strange, the voices she had started to hear suddenly vanished until only her family's voices were in the underground sanctuary. What? but Alan was a new white mage he shouldn't have this amount of control for a few more years!

Alan noticed even if she hadn't that Hopix's skin was now a more greenish hue, plus the fact that Alan could feel her powers had increased almost double, more than almost all but one he'd met here, smiling he knew now what had to be done. Looking at Hopix, he thought of the underground sanctuary, as soon as they were there, there was a multitude of gasps. Everyone knelt before Hopix and Alan, leading Hopix to the queen. Alan saw that Hopix's eyes were filled with tears as she caressed the queen's face.

"I am sorry Hopix," Alan started, "I do not wish to cause you pain." Hopix looked at Alan in confusion, then fell to the floor screaming as Alan began to pull at her. Tears were falling from his eyes when he felt the spirits start to pull from her body.

Alan prayed his strength held out, he could feel the two minds start to separate; problem was Hopix's weakened body was starting to lose the fight. Cursing under his breath, he didn't see all the elders, and every magical being in the sanctuary also lend their power to what he was doing.

Alan decided that he didn't care, for once, just once in his life, he felt he had made a difference, opening up he began to push with everything he had, not caring if he survived as long as these two did. Finally, he felt the two completely separate one drifted and settled in the queen, the other was trying to depart, something Alan wasn't about to let happen. Anchoring her Alan saw her and called out, surprised she turned, a look of joy and something he couldn't recognize on her face.

Her spirit stopped and came to Alan, Alan, she thought, It's alright I am more than ready to go I...

NO! Alan shouted out in his thoughts, I will NOT release you, you are needed more than I ever will be!

Grabbing her he pulled her with the last of his strength. Suddenly, Queen Glimmer was there. I am proud of you both, you for keeping me alive Hopix, and you, Alan your heart is so rare that I fear the existence would end if you were to pass. Please, both of you return, there is much, very much more for both of you to accomplish. Neither of you realize just how important you are, return.

Alan helped Hopix all the way back, the queen was also helping; opening his eyes he saw that Hopix was starting to wake up. Good he thought, the queen and several others were standing over him, smiling he nodded then surrendered to the darkness there were several screams as he started to spiral downward further into the darkness, damn was that Hopix? Wow, that woman had a set of lungs.

Six days later, Alan's eyes snapped open; groaning, he tried to sit up and fell almost to the floor, huh? Almost? Looking over at the feet next to his eyes he heard a familiar voice, "It wouldn't be right for you to get hurt before you're healed," it said. Pushing, Alan righted his self sitting on the cot. "I am so glad that so many of us are free to think again; the energy has strengthened us so much that others are starting to break free of the false rulers hold. What started with a mere one hundred forty five freed slaves has grown in almost a sque to one hundred forty-five thousand!"

Alan nodded listening to her feeling his strength rapidly returning, that is 'til his stomach almost roared.

Embarrassed Alan waved his hand making food he could eat appear before him, almost ashamed to look at the queen till her stomach almost roared. The queen started to laugh, Alan snapped a look up at her as he too, started to laugh. God! It felt good he couldn't remember the last time he felt this good.

"Your Majesty," started Alan.

The queen held up her hand, "I am Glimmer to you young man, you are never to call me queen again we are equal as far as I and my people are concerned," leaning close she whispered, "Though many almost consider you a god, I have told all that you do not wish to be praised or bowed to or I'd punish them. I won't, it's just a good deterrent," she said as she smiled, a smile that reminded him the most of Hopix's. The queen turned away, Hopix had been right, he did broadcast his strongest thoughts; at least he wasn't all of them anymore, as Hopix said he was a few sques ago.

"Is Hopix safe," Alan asked. Glimmer only nodded, relieving Alan's troubled mind.

"Alright, Glimmer you know I have to confront the false ruler, I really don't want to kill her but if she is like the last one I might have no choice. I have not decided... ," stopping Alan realized that the queen was staring at him.

"What's wrong Glimmer?" He asked.

"You referred to the false ruler as she, the last was a she before he came. You will need more training to see those that mask what and who they are you your self are starting to do so."

Alan shook his head, son of a bitch! He'd let the bastard fool him, if this weak one could then he was in for a tough time with this job. It was true Hopix had helped him more than anyone he'd met, but with her home, he was pretty sure she would stay knowing her station.

Again the queen turned away though he wasn't as strong as an hour ago he was still sending out his strongest feelings. A small smile, then a tear fell from her eye she hated concealing the truth, as she knew nothing could change Hopix's mind once she made a decision.

"This changes things quite a bit but is he really as weak as I feel he is?" Alan asked

"Yes, well over a third of our people are free, the rest of the Fairixie's are well on their way, though there only those that you freed that are actually free in their minds. I don't know what or how you did it but if you could do that to the rest of them, you would again have our thanks," the queen said as she bowed to an opened mouthed Alan.

Reaching out, he felt many outside the sanctuary that weren't touched yet. Waving his arm in as big an arc as he could, he felt thousands sigh as all the crap left their minds. Again he waved his arm and again did the hat motion, suddenly, he felt a shift in the planet's energy, the queen smiled at him as Alan didn't realize that he had cleared every free mind on the planet and had hardly strained at all.

Finally eager to end this, Alan flashed to the front of the false ruler's palace/residence. Alan was reaching out to bring him there when he/ she appeared in front of him.

"Enough, you damn little freak!" Alan shouted, waving his arm. The woman's guise blew away as smoke causing the man now standing there to curse.

"Who the hell do you think you are?" The man spit out at Alan, "This is my world now! I control all these pathetic magical bitches!"

Alan shook his head and waved his hand at the man, suddenly frozen the man's wild eyes were looking everywhere. Just as suddenly, a huge number of the Farixies started to attack him, growling Alan could see the strands coming from the man.

Making a scissors motion, Alan began to saw away at all the strands at once, now the man was starting to sweat. Finally, a few minutes later Alan severed the last of the strands, the man's eyes were wide as he felt the last of the power he'd stolen fade.

From what Alan could feel, he was almost an average human now; too bad he couldn't or could he? Looking closer then closer still, Alan saw myriad colors coming from the man. Reaching in, he saw that the colors were coming from a never used section of the brain, hmmm wonder what it'd take to turn it off, maybe plug it? Alan imagined a plug made of the same material that the colors were coming from; holding as steady as he could, Alan began to force the plug into the area. The more it was covered, the less magic he felt from the man until he had it completely plugged, making the plug grow into the brain he felt nothing else, no magic, no pressure.

Releasing the man the man stared wide-eyed at Alan, "what have you done to me?" He shrieked.

"I plugged your powers," Alan said matter of factly.

"No, you son of a bitch! You've signed my death warrant, along with yours, you don't know who I serve, but you will, I wish I could be there to see you die! The problem is I am a dead man, no power, no life that's their rules."

A table of dark and evil beings appeared above the ground, a few feet away, the light council appeared.

"Nam Daed, you are ours!" The leader said as he reached out, only to find that Alan blocked him.

Pissed off, he tried to push past Alan; this time, the leader of the light council was stopping him.

"You know the rules, or should I call you by your name Luci..." the council leader started.

"NO! ENOUGH!," the red skinned leader of the

dark council shouted. "We concede; what say you, Nam Daed? With or against?"

"Think before you answer," the leader of the light council said, "With us, you could at least live."

"Live? With no fucking power? That's no life ask, your lap dog, oh that's right, he had no life before," the man looked at Alan, "You're such a fucking loser!"

"True," said Alan holding his temper, "But at least I am a living loser and not a fucking dead one like you," Alan said as he sneered at the man.

"Touche' bitch," the man said.

"It's decided," the red skinned leader of the dark council said. "Control your agent," He said, looking at the light council. "Do not interfere Alan," The gnome like creature warned Alan.

"Nam Daed, your soul now belongs to chaos, come Dead Man!" the dark council leader said; the man screamed as his spirit was ripped from the body and then consumed by all on the council. "Be warned, Alan Glanto, we are watching you we will not be as kind next time."

"Oh shut up Luci..." the gnome started.

"NO, we agreed not to use proper names either way, again we concede we will no longer target your agent, but we will still be watching you, having freed but two worlds, though the fairixies world was a bonus, still hasn't turned the balance in your favor." With that, the dark council vanished.

Laughing the gnome looking leader of the light council looked at Alan, "I would say you have done more than freed this world, for Lucifer to threaten, you must have really scared him. Good work, now

rest, but we'll have another for you in a few days."
With that, they were gone too.

Alan went to tell the people it was all over, but arriving in the sanctuary, he was shocked to find it empty. Looking around, he found a note with instructions to get to the queen's city.

Alan guessed that they already knew appearing in the city after an hour of flashing towards it, Alan stared in wonder at the pure crystal city. Walking toward the queens ruling building, people were running from him in terror, sighing he was afraid someone would get hurt if he didn't hurry. Entering her Palace like crystal edifice, he stopped before the throne room.

Walking in, he almost had to bend slightly to enter; there were gasps when he approached the queen. Bowing there were even more gasps but nowhere as loud as when she curtsied to Alan; several guards made a move toward Alan, he'd started to raise his hands when the queen spoke, "To everyone here, this is Alan, the mazey that has freed us, it has been many, many starons since we were free, truly free."

"Glimmer," Alan started, causing even more guards to advance Alan waved his hand, and all the guards froze where they are. "I am leaving soon, please tell Hopix I am sorry I wasn't able to tell her goodbye, I know she was so happy to be back as I am sure her grandfather must be. I cannot stay here not long, I fear the dark council is now watching me, though the light council interceded I will still have to watch out.

The queen nodded curtsying again, Alan bowed,

turned, and left.

Walking out the front of the Palace the same little girl flew to Alan and gave him a huge hug. "I knew you were good and you feel so good too, I wish you could stay but I know you have others to help as you have us."

"You never told me your name," Alan said happy he got to see her again.

"Oh," she said, "I am Glimix, 'til I turn 23 starons then I'll be free to choose my royal name."

"Royal name?" Alan asked.

"Yes, since you healed me, I can now assume my place as a princess, didn't you know?

Queen Glimmer is my mother, I just wish my sister was as serious about it as my mother and I am, after all she is 30 starons. She isn't married and has no children, sometimes I think she'll never meet a male."

Alan wasn't really listening no wonder the queen was so grateful, he'd saved the princess. "I have to go Glimix. I hope to see you again one day." Flashing out he was home in a matter of seconds, sighing he called the council.

"Yes Alan, you called?" The leader said he couldn't see them clearly and could hear them. "I am going to need another watch dog, with Hopix gone I am still in need of help," Alan said, sad and defeated, he would miss her but she was finally happy and healthy.

"Yes, Alan, we have been considering this; there will be someone here tomorrow," the leader said with a straight face, ah, these humans so simple but powerful.

Thanking them he laid down, but sleep was a long time coming, of course, this time, there were no dreams.

Alan awoke hours later rubbing his face he looked around the room, "Hopix?" he said on the outside chance she was back. Dejected he hung his head, he was glad she was back with her family but all of this seemed senseless without her, huh? Had he just thought that? I should slap myself Alan thought; where in the hell were those ideas coming from? How could he have any feelings for Hopix? They were two different species from two different worlds; shaking his head yes there was no way.

Walking to the diner this time, Alan kept his eyes open it wouldn't do to get caught unawares again for the third time. Sitting at his usual booth, Alan nodded to a police officer that came in and sat with his partner.

"Did they get a preliminary report back on that homeless guy from yesterday we found?" the first one said.

"Oh yeah, this was a weird one," the second one said, pulling a sheet of paper from his vest. "According to the M.E.'s report, the stiff had been dead for a day or two. Looks like we might be dealing with some pranksters on this one. Thing is though, can't seem to find any open graves here in the city."

"Oh great," the first one replied, "body snatching grave robbers from out of town, christ, the medias gonna have a field day with this!"

Alan ate his meal, a little shocked the man yesterday had seemed a little strange, damn it the dark council was desecrating graves now; these bastards hold nothing sacred! Alan was heading out the door when he saw another strange looking man heading his way; quickly exiting, Alan made his way to an abandoned alley. "Why are you following me? I thought I told all of you I wasn't interested, especially after yesterday! Leave me ALONE!" The man stopped short as if he'd run into a brick wall.

"You won't escape us forever! Sooner or later, you'll make a mistake, and we'll be there to feast upon your soul," The man laughed.

"Maybe one day, but not now besides, you lost one of the biggest magic user worlds yesterday. I expect to take many more before I am done!" Alan said the force of his voice knocking the man back further.

"You can try mage Alan, oh you can try!" With that the strange man vanished.

Walking back to his room, Alan sat in his chair, almost at a lost as to what to do. Suddenly there was a rush of wind then there was a shimmering of air behind him.

"You must really have the dark council worried if they are making personal appearances," the leader of the light council said. "We have another assignment for you."

"What no watchdog?" Alan threw out.

"We should have someone here when you return," The leader said. "This should be a simple one."

"Yeah right," Alan said, "You said that the first time and I had help then; what makes this so different."

"This is a simple pop in, grab the hostage, pop

out," the leader said, smiling.

"Uh huh, what is it you're not telling me?" Alan asked.

"Uh well," the leader hesitated, "The hostage is also the ruler and might be worse than the last you dealt with, although the one holding them is even worse."

"You know you guys are just fucking wonderful! You expect me to do this with no knowledge or help? What!? Have all of you completely lost your damn minds? I've been making this shit up as I went along, you have been sitting back the whole damn time safe and sound; remember, these were your mistakes not mine. I should be treated a fair sight better than I am!" Alan was screaming now his whole body was glowing a bright red, the leader had actually moved back and erected a shield.

"Alright Alan!" The leader shouted, momentarily calming Alan. "We apologize for leaving you out, you have more than proven yourself in the past. After today all information shall be shared."

With a sigh Alan tried to calm down, "Alright, I'll take a look, but after this, I won't do a thing 'til I have all the information not just some of it!"

Alan laid down and was immediately asleep; within moments, his dream self was standing, he guessed he was standing in a cloud. Looking around nothing even closely resembled anything that was familiar to him. Screw this, make everything look like something I can handle. Just as suddenly everything took on a more solid appearance, 'bout time, Alan thought. Moving forward, he saw a few buildings ahead, hmmm there were also what appeared to be quite a few guards there also.

Walking up to them, Alan saw that they were suddenly on alert; hold strange one, this is the new ruler's residence, we will not allow anyone past.

Waving his hand all of the guards were suddenly asleep, Alan kept walking 'til he was in the door way. Looking inside he saw a strange looking lizard shaped creature, lashing another tied up lizard type creature with its tongue. From what Alan could feel the restricted one was in a lot of pain, sighing, he cleared his throat.

Who are you? Ah! I see the council has sent their latest lap dog to correct their mistakes as they put it. Too bad you're going to die right here! Turning, the standing lizard shot flames (Geez! go figure huh) at Alan throwing up his arms the flames just stopped short of him. NO! You're not even here! You're the son of a bitch that killed my brother and his children! Take care lap dog, I will kill you and soon. You want this little pansy ass, here, with that the tied lizard was flying at Alan, Be warned I will not rest 'till you are dead and my brother and brethren are avenged!

With that, the other was gone in a flash, Alan sighed and tried to reach to the other still tied up when they both were drawn to ... somewhere else. Alan looked around though there wasn't much to see. Alan thought he could see a few of the council members in the distance.

"Alright I'm here!" Alan shouted, "I've brought the one you requested." Alan wasn't one to be kept waiting, the longer he had to wait the angrier he got, damn it they sent him out and were making him wait!? Ok this shit needed to stop right here, right now!

Several people approached the two men, "Alan we didn't expect you to obtain him this quickly," the leader explained, "I apologize for you having to wait."

"Yeah well, at least you could have warned me that the one who was holding him, was the brother of the first one I went against. You know a little pre-knowledge beforehand could have prepared me better before I went in there. This won't happen again or you'll be looking for another enforcer, I hope we understand better now?" Alan said, almost ready to walk out. Now that he knew when he was being used, he wasn't about to let that happen again.

"What!? You actually saw him?" they asked, "he is far more dangerous than we at first thought. For now, the planet is safe and returning to normal, though unlike the first two they aren't protected, could you return and shore it up?"

Sighing, he knew that I'd been had, why was it that they always seemed to know when he desired to actually help?

"Alright but no more going in blind, if you really want me as your enforcer or fixer, I'd better start getting more information." He said as he turned and started to leave.

"Mage Alan," he heard from behind him, "we need to give you the information."

Sighing he stopped and turned right as the leader of the council sent a beam his way that hit his head, suddenly, his mind was filled with cruelty, screams of pain and anguish, the death of quite a few then the spirit of the people there finally broken. He was feeling dismal, how in the hell was he going to help these people they'd probably see him as another cruel ruler, he could still feel their mistrust of anyone not of their kind.

Alan arrived back on the planet, he could feel the despair it was coming from everywhere; damn it, this son of a bitch had really done a number on this place.

Alan reached out to the nearest being, expecting resistance he was going to explain what he was going to do. The thing is there was no resistance, Alan tried to explain what he was going to do, but it wouldn't listen. How in the hell do you help someone who has given up all hope? Who is afraid the least resistance could spell the death of its family and planet?

Sitting Alan tried to think of some way to get through, he had magic, sure but didn't think he had enough knowledge yet to cure what was ailing these beings. Sighing Alan cleared his mind and tried to think of an answer, all got quiet around him then suddenly he was back on Horpix's planet. Alan flew forward and stood before Queen Glimmer within moments, though the guards had already tried to block him.

"Hello again, Glimmer," Alan started.

"Alan!' she said, startled, "I didn't expect to see you again so soon, what is wrong? Your face holds such a look of confusion and desperation."

Alan went on to tell her everything he could, what he'd felt and seen when he'd gone back to try and release these people. The Queen nodded thinking for a few long moments, "I think you'll need one of my people with you, they know my people there and know of us being captured. I feel it is the only way to truly free them, but who to send? So many of my people are just starting to regain their power."

Alan looked at the Queen in shock, just started to regain their power. "Ok," he started, "I'm still new at this, what do you mean they just started to regain their power?

From what I saw when I was here they had plenty of power."

Queen Glimmer's face took on a serious look as she leaned closer to him, "What you were seeing was their power forced to the surface. This had destroyed millions in the past, there are times I am still surprised that we survived at all. You did more than just free us, Alan, you gave us back life that we can never repay you."

Obviously, Alan's face held shock as the Queen looked at him and shook her head yes. "Thank you, Glimmer but I still I didn't do that much, I also thank you for your help with these people, I am near my wits end on what to do about them."

The questioning look she was giving Alan made him stop a moment, "wits end?" She questioned.

Alan smiled, "I'm sorry, it's a term on my world that means I am out of ideas about how to help them."

The Queen nodded her understanding, "I will send you someone as soon as I locate them in the meantime, go back and try to repair what you can." Nodding I thanked her and was suddenly back on the planet.

Looking around Alan saw that truly these beings had nothing. He approached the first being he saw cringing as he saw it shake at his approach. In the lowest and softest voice Alan could, he asked if any cities were left.

Immediately one of the three mouths on the face of the being spoke, "No great Tracka, this area used to be a great city when I was small, it has been gone almost all my life." Looking at the small being, Alan saw what it had as a child, hmmm, not too bad, as he turned and started to lift a building from the ground where it had been in his mind. Soon he had almost half of what he'd seen, damn this was almost fun for a change. The small, yellow skinned, four-eyed, three mouthed creature could only stare in almost disbelief.

Alan turned to the creature, "I want you to tell all your people this is where I want them to be, this is their ancient city, and I want them in it." The small creature was slowly backing away from Alan shaking, terrified to obey, yet terrified to disobey. Sighing Alan could see it would take a lot to free these people, if it was truly possible. "Please go, tell as many as you can, I want them here, many are sick the walls will protect them now."

All four eyes wide, the older creature started scrambling away to spread the word.

Sighing again Alan looked around the place it was missing something. Looking again at the vision he'd gotten from the creature, Alan snapped his fingers ah! There had been a wall! With that he began to pull, a ten foot tall stone wall began to grow from the ground around the city he'd erected, a smile crossed his face, he was glad when the wall crushed where the last cruel ruler had lived. An hour later, a few of the creatures started to top the hill; though the younger ones didn't really understand, the much older ones began to cry as they saw the last great city.

Slowly and painfully, they came to the entrance, their eyes huge at the grandeur of the ancient city that had once been their home. Though many were wary of it they had been commanded by (as they saw it) the new ruler of their planet, so they dared not to disobey. Alan had hidden out of sight, afraid they might scatter in terror if they saw him near the entrance. Well, he thought all I have to do is wait for Glimmer to send me someone, then maybe I can truly start to help these people.

CHAPTER 3

Alan stood nearby, watching as more and more people came into the old city, he'd made sure each building had food in it, more than enough for these starving beings. An hour later, almost as if on que one of the Queen's people appeared next to him.

"Hello Mazey Alan," she said, "Queen Glimmer sent me to help these beings, so you could also. It may take me a long time, I believe you call it an hour? Yes a very long time indeed. Go home and return in two of your hours, I should have opened their hearts and minds by then." Alan nodded, he was starting to feel hungry; a quick bite might help after all. Awakening on the bed it took a moment for Alan to adjust to his surroundings, it seemed like years since he was here. Stretching Alan looked at his plain room again, god he thought how far down I've fallen sighing, he realized that he missed Hopix far more than he had thought at first.

Walking out Alan headed to the same diner he'd been to the last few days he'd eaten. He was almost there when he felt several sets of eyes on him, hmmm, Alan could feel the evil and hatred oozing out of the owners all directed toward him. Stopping a moment, he didn't feel any of them come any closer to him, which was a good thing too, it was never a good time to mess with Alan when he was hungry as he tended to be more impatient and cranky. He only waited a moment and then went in, at least they were wising up then again as frustrated as he was, a good fight right now might help.

Finally, getting to eat in peace, for once, Alan could still feel them out there, and it appeared that there were more than just a few of them. What, were they that afraid that they were going to attack in mass? A bad mistake for sure he had a little surprise for them.

He was probably half way back to his room when he felt the first two, then another four, then five more steps out behind him. Better take this out of the way, Alan thought as he turned a corner and widened an alley way. He felt now a total of twenty advancing on him, shit, wasn't that a bit of over kill? Moving to the far end he awaited their eventual appearance.

All twenty had entered the alley way when Alan closed it off to the outside world. "Well, is there one to speak for all of you or are you going to get in each other's way trying to get to me?" Alan started.

"I speak for all, you have caused your last stoppage of the dark council's plans. Today you die!" The man yelled.

Laughing Alan waved his hand, freezing eighteen of the twenty men. Hmmm ok they sent two true powered ones this time, Alan thought, good I'm through playing. The two men looked at each other and laughed then advanced on Alan. Yawning Alan waited 'til they were ten feet away then grabbed both in mid stride, squeezing, both screamed until a black mist rose from each. Looking at the others they also had a mist rising from them, then all twenty bodies crumbled to dust. Shaking his head Alan had to tell the council.

Yes Alan, we saw, unfortunately though the council can no longer intervene, their agents still can, be careful you have eliminated some of their more powerful agents, but they have many more out there. The council thought.

Great, Alan thought, so now they are prying into my thoughts? Well, that kind of put a damper on anything private now didn't it?

No, Alan we have no desire to pry into your private thoughts, we are only listening now as a precaution to you being attacked and needing help. Though from all that we've seen in the last few cases you are far more advanced than we at first thought. Thought the council.

Alan was about to fire off a snapping answer when he received a message from the Fairixie he'd left on the planet.

Mazey Alan! He heard the little woman call. I have freed enough of the people that they will listen to you; many have heard my story and that of my people and wish for your help.

Alright, replied Alan, I am returning in a few moments.

Lying down, Alan was back to the planet within moments, there were a great many gasps when he appeared but at least this time, there was no whole sale screaming.

An older member of the defeated people stepped

forward, "Tracka Alan, the Fairixie has explained who and what you are. Though you have provided for our people the first comfort any have had in almost their entire lives, many are still untrusting."

Alan nodded he had been afraid when he first saw them that, many had been denied for all their lives as the elder being said.

"I am not here to rule you, I have no interest in that, I work with the light council," this garnered a few startled reactions in the crowd. "I was hoping that this gift of one of your oldest cities might help you recover better."

"Yes," the elder started, "many though, still think that you will indeed take everything soon. You are the first to actually give us a piece of our selves back, along with some of our history. For that alone I thank you, I can sense that there is more you wish to do for us."

"I wish to make sure that no one can control you like that again, something like I did for the Fairixies." Alan stated.

"That would be wonderful," started the elder, "though I am afraid many will be resistant to the idea, we will do what we can. Please start with those of us that will allow it, that way, maybe many others will follow."

Sighing Alan could see that this was going to be a long few weeks; fixing their minds would take no time at all it was just going to be difficult to get them all obviously. Working on each individual was going to take a long time, though there were a few things Alan thought he could do to speed it up a bit.

After two long weeks, Alan finally finished with

the last group of the Tribocs as he started to call them. That plus the fact he'd also raised three other cities on the planet, was also helping with the cause.

With the planet protected Alan realized that this was the first time he hadn't had to actually be there, well that was weird in a way, true he'd gone back each day to take care of his body, still it seemed he was gone from it most of the time. The council thanked him again telling him he earned a rest, nodding he was back in his room. Opening his eyes he looked around the room, sighing; he wished it wasn't so sad, damn he missed Hopix.

"And why would you miss me?" He heard near his ear turning he could barely make out her outline.

"Please don't play with me I know she went home to stay," Alan said.

"Why would I do that when you need me here so badly?" Hopix replied. Alan had to do a double take; was it really her?

Alan couldn't move, he almost dared not to breathe, he knew she'd gone home, he knew she'd been homesick for centuries. What the hell was she doing back here? His mouth must have been hanging open cause Hopix started to laugh, "What have you missed me that much Alan?" Hopix giggled.

"I thought you were gone for good! When I took you home I felt your longing to stay there." Hanging his head Alan whispered, "I thought you'd be happier there than here with me. Alright! Yes damn it! I missed you that bad ok?"

Hopix couldn't believe what she'd just heard, Alan had missed her? Why? She was just a simple Fairixie, trying to do her job for the council, to save as many as she could before Alan was either tired of the job or was killed. Just because he'd freed her planet and saved what was left of her family, she would devote the rest of her life to him.

"Alan," she breathed out, trying to control her shaky breath, "I am here to help you; many things that are wrong were my fault, such as the one that took my planet." Here she hung her head, she couldn't tell him not yet, if he wasn't ready she'd loose him forever, she'd waited far too long to allow that to happen. "I am hoping that we can set right so many wrongs done by the recruits I tried to train." Again she hung her head.

"Hopix," Alan started. "I am more than willing to help you and accept your help, we're a team and a damn good team at that."

Hopix had been hoping he would say something like that but it was still too soon for her to say anything, if she lost him right as they were getting started, she'd never recover. She'd been researching this at home the whole time after her grandfather had said what he had, or she'd have been back sooner.

"I hope so Alan, as I said there is so much to do yet, we have barely scratched the surface." Hopix almost whispered.

Alan was still slightly in shock, not only had Hopix come back but she still wanted to work with him. He still felt he was the worse mage than any of them had ever seen.

"Alan, you really have to stop thinking like that! You are truly a rare find of a mage, you are accomplishing things that haven't been seen in thousands of years."

Again Alan was a little shocked, he didn't think that his thoughts were that strong. Was Hopix actually a mind reader or was she more sensitive than most?

Hopix had to bite her lip, damn it! Her and her big mouth! She wasn't used to being this excited. As a matter of fact she wasn't this used to being as confident in her abilities as she was now. She looked at Alan a feeling of pride growing in her chest, something else she wasn't used to. What Alan had said was true, at first she had wanted to stay home with her mother and sister, god she had missed them for so long. Now thanks to Alan, she had a family again another thing that she could never truly repay him for.

"I went over a report of your last job; you did extremely well Alan," Hpoix said.

"I don't know how you think I did well, it took Queen Glimmer and your people to convince them to let me help them; not exactly a glowing review," Alan replied.

"No but, you have to think of it this way," started Hopix, "you wasted no time and found a solution within minutes of thinking of it. To me and I'm sure to them you are definitely a hero, your quick thinking saved them even more suffering."

Ok, Alan thought, when you thought of it that way he ... might have helped a bit. Hopix sighed what was she going to do with this man? It seemed he had no confidence at all, had his female partner drained it that much from him? Suddenly anger swelled in her chest, she wanted to do violent and terrible things to Alan's mate.

Shocked Hopix shook her head and then felt the dark council's icy cold tendril pull away. Hmmm trying to hurt Alan through her, crafty but wasn't going to work, sticking her tongue out at them she felt them bristle then they were gone. She had to do something to bring Alan's confidence up but nothing she thought of would really work, she'd have to work on this she sighed.

"The council has given you a few days off Alan, they think you need rest and a chance to relax. The only problem is I have no idea what people of this time enjoy, the previous selections liked different things."

Hopix could feel one of the things Alan desired above all the others, blushing she knew she couldn't supply him with THAT! Well, not yet anyway but someday she hoped to, it all depended on Alan and his feelings if any that he had for her.

"It's alright, I'm just glad I've given your people, the Slimtori, and the Tribocs a new lease on life." Alan said with a sad smile.

Hopix hated to see Alan so sad, she vowed that no matter what she would cheer him up. Again she blushed, true she hadn't in well over a thousand years, and Alan more than peeked her interest still she had to make sure of her and Alan's feelings. It wouldn't do to confess to Alan just to have him reject her, crushing her feelings forever.

Alan rested the rest of the day 'bout damn time he thought, Hopix was just glad she had him back though it killed her not to reveal her true feelings she stayed by Alan's side through the night. The next day Alan went to eat, Hopix actually went with him though no one else could see her, she was still a little afraid. Half way to the diner a shadowy figure stepped from an alley way, her eyes wide when they saw the Fairixie that was hovering close to her target.

Hmm, she thought, at least the council was using their head this time, she'd kill his ass where all the others had failed! Alan ate, watching everything that was going on, no point in going to sleep there were too many of those bastards on earth to ignore. He and Hopix had just left when he felt rather than saw the evil presence that was following him. Never subtle are they. Walking into the same alley Alan waited, telling Hopix to stay back and what he'd felt.

Moments later a gorgeous woman walked around the corner, and immediately Alan sealed the alley way.

"I don't know why you idiots keep trying to get me to switch sides, it ain't gonna happen!" Alan shouted, his anger rising.

The woman in front of him mouth dropped open, he was on earth! There was no way he had control of his power! "We no longer wish to get you to switch! You are now targeted for DEATH!" She screamed as she shot (go figure) a fire ball at him.

Extremely pissed off they were now trying to kill him, Hopix noticed that he was glowing brighter than ever before, but how? This planet always dampened all magic, it had for centuries! Yelling no, the fireball bounced back at the woman, screaming she tried to stop it, then hold it.

Finally, she cursed Alan telling him he was a dead man he was only one man they would kill him soon. "You can try but right now I have a count of twenty-three to nothing; you make twenty-four bye bitch!" Alan said as the fireball engulfed the woman, then was gone as soon as her screams stopped.

Taking a deep breath, Alan tried to calm down still not noticing his skin was glowing an intense reddish blue color. Hopix was startled she had to contact the council as soon as she could, in all the thousands of years she'd been doing this she'd never seen a human express his power visually while on earth. Smiling she thought it had to be Alan, he was the most unusual human she'd ever met or ... shaking her head no! He couldn't be! There was no way! Sighing she could see she would have to take another trip home too; things were starting to get stranger by the moment.

They'd both just gotten in to his room when the light council contacted them. "Alan please forgive us but we have a case that we need you on, it appears that this planet is about to die. It has been drained to the point that the core has started to destabilize. It also appears to be the same one you met on the last planet, do you think you are rested enough to face him?"

Alan thought for a moment, feeling his strength, "I believe I am; though not as strong as his brother, he is still powerful enough to harm a great many." Alan replied.

"Good, please leave at once," the council ordered.

Alan laid down, Hopix flying to his side, "be careful Alan, this one is far smarter than his brother, plus I feel that he will have many escape plans."

Alan nodded, lying down he closed his eyes and reached out for a planet like a council had described. Within moments he was there, the sky was dark, the air foul. Reaching out Alan found the source of all the planet's distress.

Again Alan felt the same entity that he had on the Tribocs planet. Reaching deep Alan powered up as much as he could, his anger also building. Releasing it he sent as big a fist shape charge at the entity as he could. He felt the other crumple from the onslaught almost all the energy fleeing back into the planet.

Appearing next to the again lizard shaped magic user, Alan reached in, crushing his shape shifting ability. The lizard creature screamed looking at Alan, again Alan crushed two, then three, and then a fourth ability before the lizard's eyes got huge and he flashed out. Damn it! Hopix had warned me, but I was so anxious to stop him I let him escape; at least he can never do this again.

Nor can he feed off others, but the other two abilities Alan was unsure of. Alan reached out, feeling all the beings on the planet close to death, freezing all of it, Alan tried to accelerate the energy feeding back into the planet, and finally the planet started to feel more like it should.

Releasing all the life was harder than he thought; within moments, a massive amount of green fuzzy life forms were crowded around him. Alan, though tired, had to make this planet safe, extending, he first protected the core, then the beings.

They all stared at Alan with wide eyes then they all bowed, "We thank you, Tranzarie no other has ever shown the caring and compassion that you have. If you ever have need of us, you forever have an ally and friend in all of us." the leader said.

"May I ask what you call yourselves? Alan asked, feeling a little stupid asking but had been taught if you didn't know ask there was always power in knowledge.

"Yes Tranzarie, we are called Trembly," the leader replied. "We will raise an effigy to you so that all will know that we are not alone that at least one being cares for us."

"I do not like to be praised as a god that I am not, at present I am trying to stop many with power like me who think they are." Alan explained.

"Yes, we have sensed this, take this," the leader handed a box to Alan ... which fell through his hand. Again there were a great many gasps. Many withdrew in awe, "you ... aren't really here are you?"

"No, I am still on my planet, though I do wish to help as many as I can I am not always truly there." Alan said.

The leader bowed, "we respect your wishes Tranzarie when you can we would greatly love a chance to actually meet you. When you depart this will follow you and be near you, it has a great many more benefits than just travel. Please be well Tranzarie."

Alan just blinked, ok where was the fight? The suffering he had to ease? This was an unusual case. There was nothing that he's gone through in the first three cases he'd been on. Still unable to move Alan just stood there waiting there had to be something that he'd missed. The cases were never that easy, and to win the love of a people for really doing nothing but showing that he cared? Alright he thought what the trick was! Nothing was ever that easy especially for me! Suddenly Alan felt a tug and was opening his eyes on the bed in his room.

"How was it?" Hopix asked as soon as he appeared.

"Something is going on." Alan said, "I've never had a case go that easily!"

A moment later, he summoned the council, "Alright, what the hell is going on?" They all looked at Alan with questioning looks, I've never had an easy case." He then proceeded to tell the council everything that had happened.

"Wait," the elder spoke up, "you actually entered his mind and crushed his abilities?"

"Yes. I thought that's what I said, he can't change form anymore he's a lizard 'til I let him change, he can't absorb power anymore. The other two I'm unsure of I made sure they wouldn't come back I sealed them after I broke them.

All of the council members were sitting there with open mouths, they'd thought it a fluke when Alan had done it to the man on Hopix's world but for him actually to do it in a battle was far more impressive.

"Also I set the core of the Trembly world so that it could not be hurt again." Alan said.

Again the council members were amazed not only had he defeated the lizard man, taken some of his power but the Trembly had actually spoken to Alan an unheard of thing! A moment later the multicolored box appeared next to Alan.

"Oh yeah, they also gave me this and wish to actually meet me some time, I told them I would when I can."

Hopix's heart swelled with pride, she knew when she'd found him that he was special, but it wasn't 'til now that she realized just how special he truly was. The council all stared in dumbstruck appreciation of Alan's control block, a block that could let Alan go anywhere he desired, even the few thousand of blocked worlds. It had been no wonder the dark council had attacked the Trembly world.

Alan held the cube in his hands, feeling all the love and compassion that had been poured into it. He was about to set it down when he heard a weak call for help, huh? Looking around, he thought he heard it again.

"I've heard a call for help," Alan said, "I don't know how to use this yet nor..." Alan felt a short shock then he could see where the call was coming from. "I can see it, I can see the people, and they look so much like Hopix and her people; though they are very pale in color, paler than even Hopix was."

Hopix's eyes grew large, but how? No one had heard anything from that planet in over five thousand years she should know she'd sent her younger brother to investigate. If it were true, perhaps her family could be whole again. Tears began to fall from her face she hoped it was true she had missed her brother fiercely.

Alan stood transfixed, staring at the cube and seeing scenes that only he could see playing before his eyes. Moving closer, Hopix touched Alan's shoulder suddenly, she was immersed in the same images standing next to Alan.

"My god!" Whispered Hopix, "it's our sister planet, so far away."

Alan turned to stare at Hopix he could see her staring in sadness at the ruin and decay. Suddenly they both heard a small cry for help, rapidly they were drawn to where the voice had come from. The council was all opened mouth again Alan saw a blocked word? Was it possible that they had given him the power to go there?

Rushing forward they came upon a younger looking version of Hopix. Hopix gasp, "that's my brother he's hurt."

The council looked at Alan, "you can obviously go there but you are on your own Alan, we lost any chance of helping the people there centuries ago. If you free enough of them we will then be able to intervene, but not 'til then. We wish you well and success, you go in blind as we have no information about this place."

Alan just nodded, then turned, "I realize this but this was a genuine cry for help that I cannot ignore, if I can free the world, I will, if not, then I will leave it with those that wish to leave. Please be ready either way, we both know that the dark council is upset over losing those four worlds I feel Hopix's world would have given them an advantage that might not have been overcome. They know I have the cube, and I feel they are preparing for my arrival."

The entire council nodded, each impressed with Alan's desire to free all that he could on the sister world. Looking at Hopix he nodded, "I'll bring him home if I can, know this," Hopix nodded and threw her arms around Alan's neck, tears falling freely and unashamedly. Then Alan touched his other hand to the cube and was gone.

Oh my god! Hopix thought he actually went there! Hopix knew that the Trembly was powerful, but she didn't think they were that powerful! I have to do something she thought, thinking of the last place he'd gone Hopix concentrated 'til she was standing on the surface of the planet. Her mouth opened in amazement it was beautiful! She sat not sure what to do or who to talk to. She smiled at many of the flowers using her magic to bring them fully into bloom. They were so lovely!

The beings here must love them, no longer concentrating she started to bring as many of the flowers to bloom as she could, the aroma was so good she just couldn't stop. About this time, she noticed quite a few of the green fuzzy beings watching her. Suddenly afraid, she went to the elder, "Elder sir, I wish to apologize to you and your people for bringing your flowers out early. They were so lovely and I thought I'd try to make it more beautiful for you and them. I meant no harm, I am not thinking clearly."

"Little one," the elder started, "never in our history have we had a powerful magical being help us, and in the same day another powerful magical being apologize to us. Tell me little one, are you acquainted with the Tranzarie Alan?"

Hopix mouth dropped open, she was just trying to help a habit she'd gotten from Alan, how did they know?

Bowing Hopix nodded and said, "Yes, elder, I am

his magic watchdog for the council."

"Ah! I see! You had a chance to go home yet you came back to Tranzarie Alan, how long have you had a room in your heart for him?"

Again Hopix could only stare opened mouthed, no one knew! "I don't..."

The elder chuckled, "be still little one, to us, emotions are nothing to feel and read, it is how we truly know when a being means us harm or not. Now then, why are you here, and don't worry you actually helped, Alan forgot the flowers when he saved us all, a minor point compared to all the other life here."

"I am worried elder, Alan has gone to the sister world of my planet, and my brother is there. The council has no knowledge of it, as the dark council has blocked it for a long time." Hopix said still worried about Alan.

"I feel Alan is more ready than you think, the cube helps him to focus and think clearer he will be fine, but he needs you, little one, don't think he doesn't, and don't wait too long before you tell him or the secret of your people."

Again Hopix could only stare at the elder.

Alan appeared on an open field; nothing seemed to be alive. Even as he stood there a small squad of Fairixies moved in to attack him, it was almost the same as before.

Reaching out he caught the leader wrapping her tight he saw she was just as the one's on Hopix's world had been, clearing her mind then blocking outside control she looked up at Alan, "Where am I?" then her eyes grew large, "Please protect me," she begged.

Damn here we go again, Alan thought.

Alan pulled the leader of the squad inside his shield, the squad though confused continued its onslaught. Not wanting to play with them all day, Alan let loose a blast knocking all of the squad out, clearing their minds, and blocking all outside thoughts.

Alan had reached the last one when the Fairixie stared straight at Alan, "You think you're so damn righteous don't you ass hole? You're gonna learn what real damn pain is, there are ten of us on this planet. You should remember that you might get one or two, but you won't get all of us! I'll so enjoy your damn death, you sack of shit!" Then the voice was gone. The woman stared at Alan after he cleared her mind and blocked everything.

"What have you done?" She screamed, "I can't hear my master!"

Shit, he'd been afraid of this; snapping his fingers, he brought all but the one within the shield.

"I don't know how you can call THAT a master, a cruel, torturing, non-caring ass. He cares nothing for you, he has you fooled." Alan threw at the Fairixie.

"No you're wrong master loves me, cares for me as he does all of us." The woman shouted back.

Several of the Fairixies with Alan shouted at her that she was a fool; all he'd done was torture them and take their powers. The lone woman's eyes got huge, but she still refused to relent in her position then flew off.

Looking at the group of scared and shaking women, Alan asked if they had a safe place to go.

Alan said he'd make it bigger and stronger when they answered yes, but it was small, and only a few could go therr. Arriving, they were met with several shrill screams; many there were trying to hide.

The leader stepped away from Alan, telling all there what Alan had done for them, how they were free of the voices, and that Alan said that the voices would never be there again. Finally, things calmed down Alan again was enraged that the peace loving Fairixies were being tortured, subjected to horrors of the mind and body that Alan was sure would have drove him crazy long before now.

Reaching out Alan first enlarged the area they were living in, this of course brought out concern that now they would be an easier target. Alan just shook his head no and started to strengthen the weak shield around the area. Next he went to each of the wounded, trying to heal all the physical wounds first. Huh the last time this had worn him out so quickly, was this the advantage to actually being here?

Shaking his head he still couldn't believe that they had harmed the children. Hours later, Alan was completely done when they all heard an angry buzzing sound, at one of the openings two squads began to pour in ready to? All of them stopped as soon as they were inside, the confusion on their faces apparent. Alan quickly seized them all clearing their minds then blocking all outside influence.

A few of those that had just come in began to scream like the one from before, damn it thought Alan just how stupid are these people? Snapping his fingers, the five who had complained were outside the safe area. "I don't think he'll send anymore to attack here," Alan said, sighing. Alan could see he need to expand again, as he did he felt another safe area not all that far away. Opening a through way Alan soon had both areas connected though he'd actually have to go to the other to strengthen it. The same squad leader said that she would take him after she returned. The woman left down the new tunnel Alan had dug, reappearing in less than five minutes with an elder.

"She has told me you are a Mazey, that you were on the great home planet of all Fairixies, is this true?" Alan nodded and stared into the eyes of the elder. Tears began to flow from his eyes, "ah Queen Glimmer is as beautiful as she was when we left. Please come help, I can already feel the spirit of our people so strong here. If we have enough of this, we can defeat the ten deadly masters."

Alan nodded he was going to do all he could though there were ten he knew that there was a way to defeat them. Sighing he just had to find it smirking he also thought yeah and survive.

Emerging outside the area, Alan surrounded himself and the elder with a shield, slowly they made their way almost another mile across the twisted dying landscape. Finally, pissed off Alan stopped the elder, "I have to repair this," waving his hand he saw how it was, then how it should be within a few moments the air cleared, color returned to the land.

The elder smiled, ah! He hadn't seen this since they had arrived. Going further they had almost reached the next sanctuary when more squads attacked, how many he wasn't sure. Hmmm, so they thought they could over power him huh? Reaching out Alan was through playing with these guys, a huge wave flowed from him shocking all the Fairixies.

Alan had to hurry knowing that they would recover quickly. Damn there had to be over two hundred here; the last two were clearing when a different voice came from them. "So, you are really here, we were warned that you might try to re-take this world. Come we await and welcome you to try, once you are dead and your power ours, nothing will stand in our way!" Alan smiled it was this type of bragging that the one on Hopix's world had spouted, pathetic.

"Well, you can try that's all I have to say, but even with ten of you I doubt you could win. Especially with all that I have freed. The less you have command of, the less power you have; you really don't have any power of your own!" Alan sneered.

Enraged, (not again) fireballs started to fly at Alan. Alan had learned since last time, opening a portal in front of his shield, he heard screams on the other side. Smiling Alan thought that was one less to worry about even if it didn't kill him it would render him unable to do much. Moments later all the squads awoke, looking around they all seemed lost. Well, all but ten of them, those he isolated together, sighing when they started to scream at him. The rest of them Alan pulled within his shield, most were staring at the elder and Alan. As they all started to bow to Alan, he shook his head. "Do not bow, I am not a god!"

One of the women staring at the ground started to whisper, "You are Mazey, and you are to be bowed to and served."

"No, I am not like the others, I am here to free your people," Alan stated.

Several of the women looked up at Alan, then at the elder who was shaking his head yes.

Starting to walk again, Alan and the others arrived at the second sanctuary. Waving his hand, they all appeared within the confines of the sanctuary. Again there was a lot of screaming and Fairixies scurrying to hide from him. Even with the Elder there, there were still too afraid to come out. Shaking his head and for the moment isolated, Alan stretched out his arms feeling the shield defenses. Pushing, he soon had them enlarged, next he began to expand the interior of the hide away, walking around again he found a young being the others had abandoned when they fled.

More angry than he could believe, he looked at the twisted, burnt, suffering little girl. Trying to calm his self again, there was more screaming as his hands began to glow. Not caring, Alan stooped over the little girl, Alan could see the fear in her eyes, but more than anything else he saw the horrible pain she was going through. Holding her hand, Alan's tears began to flow from his eyes, this in turn caused the little girl to no longer fear him, trying to lift her hand she whispered, "It's ok great Mazey, it doesn't hurt that much, I will be fine please don't cry."

Suddenly the little girl's skin began to glow then started to clear the little girl looked up at Alan in surprise. Then her broken arm straightened and was whole again; the little girl was shocked, Alan looked deep into her eyes seeing a sparkle appear that hadn't been there before. Alan saw the elder approach keeping the rest back, staring in disbelief at the wonders Alan was accomplishing. Finally, a mere twenty minutes later the little girl sat up her eyes opened wide, throwing her arms around Alan, she whispered a heartfelt thank you then kissed him on the cheek.

"Please cheer up now, great Mazey, also if you can, my friends were hurt though not as bad as I was. I tried to stop the bad Mazey from hurting them, so I didn't mind when he hurt me as long as he stopped hurting them."

Again tears fell freely from his eyes, god, he thought, I wish I had half the courage she does.

Following her, they went further back in the sanctuary, in another room dozens of children were hurt along with quite a few adults.

Again Alan's ire grew 'til his hands were glowing, kneeling he started to heal them two at a time, often staying in one place for almost a half an hour.

Many sat up startled, many thought they'd never walk nor fly again forever in pain from twisted and broken limbs. Finally all of them were healed, Alan felt tired, a good tired he finally felt he was truly helping. Sitting he leaned against the wall fighting the urge to sleep, he'd helped them sure but that was no guarantee they wouldn't attack him if he fell asleep. The elder floated over to him, "Sleep Mazey you are safe, and no one will attack you."

Nodding Alan drifted off, soon he was back in his room, Hopix turned staring at him her tear streaked face more than standing out to him." I have freed many but nowhere near enough yet; this world is much bigger than yours. I will return when I can Hopix." Alan told her.

"Please be careful Alan, the ten sound extremely dangerous," Hopix stated.

"Well nine of them, I've already taken one out of the picture, he won't bother me after I burned him." Alan told her.

From behind him he heard the council, "that's good though you still have the other nine," the council leader said.

"Yes, that may be true, but if you remember, they're rarely together or for another. That I believe is the way to defeat them." Alan responded.

The council leader nodded, "Remember though a common enemy, can sometimes forge alliances that otherwise would have never been."

Alan also nodded this was one thing he hadn't thought of, was he enough of a threat to all of them, then yes he could see them uniting to stop him.

Alan jerked awake a few hours later laying there he listened to the now happy sounding children. Many of the adults were still in shock hardly believing that a Mazey would help and heal; they always killed each other and hurt everyone else to instill fear. Alan just shook his head sadly, to be judged before he even arrived, did all the Mages, Wizards act like this?

Christ they were giving the few good ones a really bad name. Still almost afraid to move he needed to find out everything he could about the other nine before he tried to go against them. Thinking hopefully they would make this more interesting, Alan just hoped that not all of these idiots only used fire balls. It was more than easy to defend against them now. Looking at his heads at least now he knew why so many were afraid of him.

So that was what a physical manifestation of the power looked like, he had to remember that, thing is though why had it appeared then? He'd brought his power up and concentrated it but he'd done that before and hadn't noticed anything. Talking to the elder Alan decided he needed to go after the other nine deadly masters as the elder called them, before they united and decided to come after him. Alan reached out feeling the ten distinct areas of power on the world, cold, dark, evil power, well nine; one wasn't even half as strong as the others.

Rising out of the sanctuary Alan started toward the nearest dark power. Obviously, the masters had been warned and kept all the squads away from him. The problem was Alan thought he might have chosen the strongest of those left, hell it was just they were the closest. After a few miles the power started to grow stronger or so it hoped to fool Alan into thinking. Stopping before an ominous, dark building, seemingly growing from the ground, Alan felt the power shift. 'Oh great Alan' thought, 'they're using the Fairixies again.

Opening his senses all the way Alan was aware long before that the supposed master was trying to ambush him. Standing still Alan felt them moving slowly, whirling one hundred eighty degrees, Alan blocked several bolts of electricity, and (finally!) shaking his hand Alan smiled. Well at least this one is more interesting, a moment later Alan wasn't sure what it was that crawled from the dead bushes behind him. All Alan knew for sure was it had no legs, was grey, with several eyes on the surface, almost like a moving jello?

So you survived the bolt attack, hmm try this! The moving mass said, shooting an acid like substance at him. Alan nodded his head better, then his face screwed into a look of rage, for all you have done to these people you will die! Alan thought at the mass.

Laughing, an almost tentacle like appendage pointed at Alan, I don't think so mazey Alan! Pissed off, Alan reached out then entered the mind of the mass he grabbed the magic center of it. Squeezing, pulling, tearing, and then finally yanking as hard as he could, Alan could feel the power of the mass fade. Noooooo!!!!!!!! What have you done? My powers you can't! It screamed in Alan's mind.

Finally, the magic center now an empty hole Alan formed the plug stuffing it in effectively shutting all power off.

You're no more, Alan told the mass watching it wither trying to crawl away and hide. Sighing Alan thought that's two Alan had just started to turn when a (not again) fireball flew by his arm. Holy shit! That actually hurt! Increasing his shields wasn't that easy, the pain in his right arm was radiating into his shoulder and back. Son of a bitch! Forgot about the other eight!

"You get him?" the dark, twisted, human shape

said.

"Not sure, I hit something," the tall, what appeared to be a long legged bird said.

"We have to be sure," A black cloud like entity said, "I'm uncertain what he did to Groc, hell wasn't even close, and with Thront out of commission, that's a lot of territory open now. As long as this asshole is loose, there's a chance he could kill us. Just remember what the council said he..."

"I don't give a shit what the council said! This son of a bitch is mine, his soul is mine," turning she looked at the other two with a menacing look. "Don't get in my way!"

"Damn it Thara! If they come after you it's your ass then! Just remember right now, when he kills your ass, you DID have help.

Laughing the black cloud said, "You don't anymore." With that the cloud and twisted looking human flashed out.

Cautiously the female bird entity crept closer, finally where he had been she saw that he was long gone. "Damn it!" Concentrating she sent out a message, Asshole, yeah you Mazey you may have gotten two of us but we're ready now. I will enjoy eating your soul. I wait for you to gather the courage to come after me, here she paused and laughed, If you even dare!

Alan appeared not far from where he'd been, his abilities weren't working that well neither was his damn arm. Thinking of the sanctuary he again tried to flash out, by his estimate he made it half way there. Sweat was starting to form on his brow as the amount of pain was increasing; I have to make it he thought.

Again Alan thought of the closest sanctuary, pushing with everything he had he again flashed out this time appearing next to the opening to the sanctuary. Alan smiled he'd made it! Then the strain on him from the amount of energy he'd had to use hit him. Stumbling forward he started to feel light headed, looking at the opening again Alan thought I am going to die here.

Again he tried to move forward, the effort was draining what energy he had left, damn his arm was killing him. Finally, he grasped the edge at the hole trying to pull himself into it. Alan was fighting harder than he'd ever fought to keep his eyes open, darkness started to descend.

Well I tried, Alan thought, at least two of those murderers were gone now. Sighing he suddenly felt hands, it felt like dozens of hands pushing, pulling, whatever they could to get him inside. Why, Alan thought, they were so afraid of him. His last thought was of being carried to a bed, well at least I'm going to die in comfort he thought, then nothing.

Hopix returned back to Alan's room, more worried than she'd been to date what Alan was doing was dangerous, courageous, and absolutely crazy. All she could think of, was that he could die alone, never knowing, thinking no one else cared. Holding the cube close to her breast, Hopix thought of all the elder had said. Looking at the cube the elder had said that when she needed to use it she could, it was much more than a travel aid, so much more.

Hopix had stared at the elder, when she needed

it? Sighing she thought can't the older generation ever NOT be cryptic? As old as she was, and they still treated her like a young one, at times it infuriated her but only at times.

She sat to wait on Alan's return working up the report she would have to file for Alan after all this was over. She'd gotten through the first of it, the visit to the Trembly's, the strange visions. She'd just started on the rest when the cube started to glow, huh? She'd never seen a cube glow before what was going on. Picking it up she suddenly started to see visions like Alan had; she saw him save the first few, the sanctuary, and the second sanctuary.

Then she saw the fight with the horrible creature, she felt Alan start to relax his shields. That's when she saw the other three screaming at Alan that there were three more behind him. Even as she watched in horror, Alan started to turn, she was glad he had, or the fireball would have hurt him seriously. As it was, the damn thing got half way through seriously singeing his right arm.

"NO ALAN!" Hopix screamed, watching Alan flash out three times the last short of the sanctuary. I have to help him, Hopix said to herself. The cube began to glow; next thing she knew, she was beside Alan. To her amazement several Fairixies appeared staring at her with open mouths, ignoring them Hopix tried to get Alan in the sanctuary, she was starting to get frustrated when finally the rest got Alan into the safe area.

The elder could only stare at Hopix, by the great queen she looked familiar, but he couldn't place where he'd seen her before. She appeared to be young only about four to five- thousand years old she'd have been young when they left so long ago. They'd gotten the Mazey in safely, the elder had heard that two of the bad Mazeys were no longer controlling their areas. This was a good thing for the moment but they had to act on it soon, for that they needed Mazey Alan.

He watched the Fairixie that had appeared near the Mazey as she kneeled next to him. What was she doing, the elder thought? His mouth dropped agape, she was a healer! This could only mean ... no! He wasn't about to get his hopes up. Hopix extended her hands trying to relieve the pain this didn't help, reaching in his head Hopix entered his dream.

"Alan," she called his dream self, "you have to start healing yourself. You were hurt in a sneak attack."

"Huh?" he said looking up. "I was wondering where you were."

"Just start healing yourself ok? I can't heal you enough, only you can." she told him. Sighing Alan said, "Alright, but you have to be there when I wake up ok?"

"I will be," she replied, "I will be."

PART 2

CHAPTER 1

Hopix was exhausted. She'd healed Alan for almost an hour, though she felt she'd barely given him the energy to recover. She laid her head down, she'd not felt this tired in over a thousand years. Alan had to fight this; he was far stronger than she thought. She fought the sleep for hours, accepting food once from a small friendly child who hugged Hopix, startling her. At that moment, Hopix felt the wonderful love and power that Alan had poured into her to heal her.

Leaning close the little girl whispered, "I am so glad that you both have come to help us, I was afraid when I first saw Mazey Alan, then he did something I've never seen a Mazey do." Hopix looked up suddenly more interested. "He started to cry when he saw all the hurts I had, I told him it didn't hurt that bad anymore, not to cry but he did even more. That's when I knew he was a good Mazey; then his hands started to glow as my skin did, and the pain was gone!" Hopix could only nod in amazement when the little girl left.

The elder again was amazed another part was fulfilled but he'd seen things like this before he still had to be sure. Walking over to Hopix he nodded to her, "Please sleep, young one, you'll be safe, no one will harm you here." Hopix looked into the elder's eyes and then closed hers, though at first, she had a hard time actually falling asleep.

Alan's head and arm were throbbing more than he thought they should be, and what a funny dream. He'd seen Hopix. Damn, he thought, don't know if I'll ever see her again the way things are going. Straining he tried to open his eyes. Crap, he was obviously hur t worse than he had at first thought. Finally, he managed to get one eye open. What the??? He was back in the sanctuary. The last thing he remembered he'd tried to flash into the place but only made it to the damn door.

Then the biggest shock came when, after a few minutes, he managed to turn his head and caught sight of Hopix! Concentrating he could feel all his wounds, they were not far from killing him. Crap, with what he could muster he first eliminated the infection, then almost all of the swelling. Not as far as he wanted to get, but now at least it wouldn't kill him while he slept. Issuing a squeak like groan to Hopix, he tried to sit up but only caused his head to spin more damn! Finally unable to keep his eyes open, he sank back into the welcome embrace of unconsciousness.

Hopix had felt him awaken then start the healing process, good all the infection was gone, then she felt him remove almost all the swelling. Damn it! He was still so weak! As he fell asleep Hopix could feel most of the tension his body had been fighting ease then fade. Good at least now he could sleep better, that in itself would help with his healing. Sighing she got up and started to add her energy to Alan, now at least she could remove some of the wounds. For another hour, she slowly removed the burns on his arm and shoulder, though she only was able to heal half of it he wouldn't have to expend as much energy when he woke up again.

The Elder sat near both of his guests, sighing he hoped that all the signs he was getting were true. It had been so long since his people had been free or even felt free. Going over all the parts of the legend it was true they were only the second to make it this far, a better sign in itself, still he didn't want to mention anything. It wouldn't do to get his people's hope's up again just to have them crushed by another charlatan.

Neither Alan nor Hopix slept well; Alan kept replaying the battle with the last two, the ass kicking he got when they appeared. I'll never be caught off guard again, when I see her again, I guarantee next time we meet that bitch is dead! Hopix's dreams were no better seeing Alan getting hurt had cut her deeply she was supposed to watch over him. Hell lot of good that had done! Now there was a good chance he could die and she was so weak she couldn't do a damn thing!

Many people were also watching the woman who appeared to be one of them and the Mazey who had healed so many who had no hope of ever being whole again. Several hours later Alan jerked awake, though most of the pain was gone the stiffness was still there. Well, at least my strength has returned he thought, sitting up there was a gasp from many there in the sanctuary, then it was Alan's turn to gasp, lying on a small pallet next to him was Hopix!

Holy shit! He really hadn't imagined it! Groaning Alan sat up, crap, I can hardly move he thought, concentrating a moment Alan's hands began to glow though not as intense as before. Finally, after several minutes the stiffness started to fade, as did the weak feeling. Ah good, now he was starting to feel like his self. Standing a little shaky, he walked to Hopix with a broad smile.

"I thought I'd never see you again," he whispered. "I thought when I left it was the last time we'd ever be together, how did you get here?" he said more to himself than to anyone else.

"I visited the Trembly as you did; they also gave me a cube like yours." Hopix said snapping her eyes open, a huge smile on her face. God she was glad to see him awake and feeling better! "Alan you have to be more careful, just like you told the council you are the one thing that they all will unite together to fight. I was so... ," Hopix started.

"Yes I know Hopix, I've already changed my plan of attack, they might unite to fight me but I can feel that they won't stay that way long. Besides with two of them out of the picture, I'm sure they are about to start fighting over those two areas." Alan told her. "Right now I have to figure a way to defeat them. Like you said I start taking them out, yes they are going to combine forces then we'll really be in trouble."

Hopix herself had been thinking on the problem, "Alan, you do realize that the more of the people you release from them the weaker they get."

"Yes, but on this world, there are far more people than there were on your planet. Plus, there are right more of them gunning for me." Alan stopped; the look of confusion on Hopix's face almost had him laughing.

"Gunning for you?" She said.

"Oh, sorry it is an expression on earth it means they are out to get me, to destroy or get rid of me." Alan explained.

Hopix just shook her head she was slowly starting to get some of the terms down; it seemed that the humans come up with more every thirty or forty of their years. It seemed to be almost madness trying to keep up with the different terms! Though he hadn't meant to, Alan still had to chuckle a little at the look on her face. When she looked at him startled, he again tried to hide it but she just stared at him with he hands on her hips a stern look on her face.

"Ok, ok, I'm sorry, but you look so damn cute when you do that." Alan admitted still smiling. Though she held back a sly smile, she did love seeing him smile. Sighing she thought it was hard to stay mad at Alan for long. "I have to get back out there as soon as possible, but I seem to be at the end of my energy."

"You were injured far worse than you thought, I tried to heal you but your power has risen. You are to a point now that my healing of you takes far longer than you usually have the time for." Hopix said a little upset as she looked lovingly at Alan.

Alan and Hopix spent the rest of the day doing what they could for all those there. Many had never been to themselves and were finding it difficult to cope without the voices in their head. Hours later, Alan was finally starting to feel more like his self.

The elder stepped up to talk to Alan drawing him to a private area to talk to both of them. "Great Mazey Alan, we have heard that you defeated two of the evil Mazey's, though this

is good for right now, we must act quickly. Though there are less of them they still control a great many of the people here, please Mazey Alan free them."

Rising from the sanctuary Alan reached out feeling for the bird woman 'til he found her, this one he thought, I will take care of first. She was the first to block me, never again! Slowly Alan and Hopix made their way across the land healing it as they went, finally, they stood outside a huge dark crystalline appearing building.

"So I see that you have more to you than I thought, come and get me!" she screamed.

"I've got a better idea," Alan said. Reaching out Alan aimed and blew a section of the building loose. "Bring your ass out here before I level this piece of crap!" Alan yelled as he took another section of the building.

Alan could feel her long before she appeared, behind him a female voice stated, "The name is Thara; unfortunately for you it is the last you will hear!" A high wind rose threating to blow everything away, Alan yawned and waved his hand behind him.

Smiling he heard the choking start, "I have to thank you bitch! I am now more than ready to take you all down; thanks to you I won't be surprised again." Extending his arm Alan caught the black cloud creature ripping it apart amid horrible inhuman screaming.

Thara tried to flash out the look of surprise and fear apparent on her face but found she was too tightly held to escape. "You bastard! What gives you the right to interfere? This is our planet, you son of a bitch!" Thara was screaming.

Alan reached in and began to strip all her powers away, each producing a deafening scream from her. Alan had almost finished when he felt another presence, throwing up another shield; the dark twisted human was firing electric bolts at him.

Smiling Alan thought hmmm, this one is actually smart. Dividing his attention between the two should have been harder than it was but as Alan found it was not even a chore. With a final tug Alan ripped the last of her magical abilities loose. Freezing her, Alan turned his attention to the last of the three.

"So, an actual woman this time, at least you have more brains than the others, a shame it won't do you much good!" Alan sneered.

"As if a lap dog man of the white council could defeat me!" The twisted human yelled. With that, she started in on a renewed campaign of fireballs (again!) electric bolts, and water waves.

"Face it bitch! You're far too weak; you're going to die for nothing!" Alan was shouting as he began to press forward with increasing strength. "Come on give up! You want to be a useless non-magic user like Thara? Yes, I took all of her power! You're next!"

The human screamed and started to press back against Alan. Surprising him a moment, she backed him back up a few steps until he felt her start to falter. Dam it! Why doesn't she give up! Ah! I see! From well behind him a new threat appeared, freezing the now startled dark twisted human, Alan turned to face the new threat.

Hopix had remained hidden the whole time scanning the area for any other threats, several of the bolts and fireballs had gotten close but nothing she couldn't handle. The appearance of the fourth Mazey had her worried a bit though, Alan had defeated two of the three that still left too many out there as of yet.

Alan could feel that this one was far different from the others he'd faced. "Hello Alan, you sorry piece of shit, tsk, tsk, I see you've been busy. One almost dead, one actually dead, two stripped of their powers, the last frozen, might as well as be dead." Here this newest addition, a short, wart covered, green skinned being snapped its fingers, the twisted human screamed as its soul was ripped from it and quickly devoured by this newest addition.

"HMMM, that's five; one of them was stronger than most of us, too bad he was so damn stupid!" Here the wart being laughed and opened its arms. "I am not here to battle you, though if I must, I will welcome an actual challenge, no, I am here to offer you a deal. We'll let you go. You can take all that you have freed with you, and we get the rest, seems fair enough, no?"

"I've got a far better deal for you, one that you should take now; this will be the only time I offer it."

Alan said in even calm tones though he felt that any minute the misshapen creature before him would soon be trying to destroy him.

"A far better deal, huh, pray do tell." the being said.

"You and the rest of your cronies can leave the planet with the few that want to be with you. I don't destroy you or them and everyone is alive. See? I have to offer you and them a far better deal than the other one." Alan said startling to clench his teeth.

"Uh huh," the being said starting to tense up. "And that would be?"

"I hunt you all down and either strip you all of your powers or I just kill you." Alan spit out.

"You can freaking try." The wart being said as it tried to freeze Alan, hmmm, that was different. Bouncing it back the other easily dodged. "I'd have thought better of you," At that moment, the other felt the blood starting to ooze from the cut on its side.

Waving a hand it flashed out, damn it, Alan thought, I'd have gotten five of them today! Reaching out Alan started to clear every Fairixie he felt, he'd done well over a thousand when a booming voice sounded.

"You have freed many but you'll never free all of them, Alan. These are our slaves, they will never all be free." The voice said.

"As I told the last one that was the only time, I would offer the deal that I did. Since he is hurt he won't be that much good to you now, there might as well be only three of you, and hell one of you is so weak I'm not sure they are worth the effort to defeat. Don't worry; you will be punished for the atrocities you have done to these people!" Alan yelled.

The voice laughed, "if you were more seasoned, I might be worried, but you are nothing, no experience, no killer instinct, HA no real power!" A huge bolt struck Alan's shield. Alan immediately sent on back the same way. A startled gasp let him know that he had found his mark. "AH! I see an actual challenge! I welcome you, you may have the areas of the dead and beaten ones."

Alan reached out and started to release every Fairixie he found. He was well over five thousand when Hopix noticed a dark cloud moving on the horizon. "Uh, Alan I think we've got trouble," she told him keeping an eye on the advancing darkness.

"It'll be alright," he told her, "those are the ones I have freed so far, and almost half of the planet is ours now."

Reaching out Alan searched the city in front of him taking all the traps and killing devices, he felt hidden all over the city. There, he thought, at least they would have a safe place for now. Almost five minutes later, the huge crowd of freed Fairixies started to bow to Alan.

"Stop!" He yelled cringing when he saw almost all the beings start shaking. In a much calmer voice, Alan started again, "My name is Alan, I am not a god, I will not make you do anything you do not want you. You are free of those that had enslaved you. This city has been cleared of everything that would hurt you, please use it." Alan turned and started to walk away,

"Alan we're being followed," Hopix said

Alan stopped and turned to see several of the

tiny beings following him and Hopix. "Can I help you further?" He asked.

"We are confused, mast ... Mazey Alan. You don't want us to do anything for you?" Several asked.

Thinking a moment, Alan couldn't see a clear way out of this, then just as suddenly, an idea formed in his head. "The only thing I can think of right now is I want you to live. Live as well and good as you can, be the best that you can be. This is Hopix. She is from the planet you all came from, talk with her. Please be well, I have to defeat the last four of the bad Mazeys. Then this planet can truly be free of the dark council." Alan explained.

Hopix shook a bit when all the eyes turned toward her. Alan kept walking he felt the one who'd gotten away not far away, huh he thought so they can't either when they are hurt. Concentrating, Alan could begin to clearly see where he was, flashing out next to him. Alan could see that he was close to death, he'd been bleeding for a bit. Shaking his head Alan thought the idiot could have been spared all this pain and death. Grabbing the wart creature by the throat, Alan slashed, and the creature was dead.

"Damn shame, you could still be alive, you idiot. All you had to have done was take the deal." Alan said to the rapidly stiffening corpse. Flashing out Alan was back with Hopix it seemed that she had finished, and the Fairixies that had been with her were happily winging their way back to the rest.

They as the rest soon learned that Alan had spoken the truth and the city was safe, there was clean water, air and food. The Elders were all weeping; the prophecy was finally starting to come true. Though many of the young didn't understand the concept of freedom, they all knew that it was a great feeling.

Appearing in the sanctuary again, Alan and Hopix started to explain about the city that Alan had cleared for them. Again, the elders here wept; many had been here for a long time and longed for the city's comfort again. Alan moved all of them to the city as soon as they were ready. Alan had well over half the planet clear now thought, the council still hadn't appeared.

They must have far more of the Fairixies within their territories than I had at first thought. Alan estimated that he'd freed somewhere in the neighborhood of over seven thousands of the beings, though that number continued to grow every few minutes. Alan reached out beyond the remaining three's boundaries; sure enough, he could feel tens of thousands still enslaved to them.

"I think it's about time I ended this," Alan said to Hopix.

"Yes, I agree, but Alan, you haven't rested or recharged, you nee... ," Hopix started.

"What I need is to finish these three off so I can free the rest of the people. I can feel their pain Hopix for the first time I can feel it. Plus the fact that we haven't found your brother yet, I promised I would find him, and I will." Alan told Hopix as they started out the front of the city. As soon as they exited, there was a harsh wind, then the same lizard being that Alan had beaten twice before flashed in.

"Hello, asshole! I do hope you remember me, it is going to be so sweet when I break you and take your little whore!" The Lizard spit out, "I await your appearance I can't wait to crush you under my feet, and then I'll have your little whore's power to make me the strongest! So hurry up I'm anxious!"

"If you are that anxious, then come to me," Alan replied.

"Oh no, this is on MY terms this time, Mine!" with that the lizard man was gone.

Wonderful, Alan thought, a damn target again. Bad enough, he knew where it was coming from, but now who also.

Alan stood there for a few moments, though the lizard guy wasn't really a challenge to him, it still amazed Alan the arrogance lizard guy had. Hopix was holding her anger in check she could feel the guy was nowhere as strong as Alan, but still he was making threats. Looking at Alan she saw he was deciding what to do, go after the stronger of the two or the lizard guy.

"I'm not sure Hopix I'm smelling an ambush in all this, I've never trusted any of the beings I've met and I'm not about to. The minute I go after the stronger ones Lizard guy will be sure to show up and try to kill me while I am weaker."

Alan stood there for fifteen minutes before finally making a decision, turning toward one of the stronger bad mages Hopix's eyes were wide. Why go after that one? It wasn't the strongest, sighing she decided she'd trust Alan he hadn't been wrong yet except when he hadn't paid attention, but Hopix felt that wasn't about to happen again.

Pulling off the ground Alan started to levitate pushing forward he reached out and healed and repaired everything he could see. Twenty minutes later they arrived at a uh ... what the hell was it, Alan thought, if he had to describe it he'd say it was a big pile of crap just thrown on the ground. Standing outside Alan reached out in all directions feeling everything. Then he took aim and blew a hole through the front of the "ugh" pile.

With a scream, the owner came flying out, damn thought Alan a pile of crap and a dung beetle. "I will kill you for what you have done!" The huge beetle screamed at him, I won't allow you to live after what you did to Groc!"

Suddenly the beetle flew straight at him. Huh, this was new. Strengthening his shield, the beetle hit it and knocked Alan on his ass! What the hell? Coming at him again, Alan caught it ... or thought he had as it started to drag him. Letting it go, he suddenly felt the lizard guy, and blasted the hell out of an entire hill side.

The screams he heard had him smiling. Ducking Alan barely avoided getting hit again. Trying to stay calm, Alan went through all the ideas that had sprung to his mind. Spray? No that was insane, what I really need is something to swat him with like a ... Alan started to smile,

"You're dead, you can't touch me while I am flying, but I can batter you 'til your unconscious. I can..." the beetle boasted, that is 'til Alan connected with a baseball bat, effectively smashing the beetle in the head." Reaching out, Alan delved in, ripping everything he could from the beetle, screaming as he felt his power fade, Alan just left him there. Reaching out he did a massive freeing of the

Fairixies.

Even with the new additions of Fairixies, the last bad guy still had over half of the population as its slaves, Alan could feel this last one was going to be a fight much like the first he'd defeated when he took the job. Alan freed another city removing everything that would kill them. Waiting he felt the approach of the large crowd. As before he told them of the city that was theirs now, it had food and shelter, they were free. Of course as they were walking away Hopix had to explain to a few hundred this time before they could truely move on.

They'd only walked for a few minutes when Hopix turned to Alan, "when this is over, there is much I need to tell you." Sighing she took a breath, Alan was staring at her a little odd. She had much to tell him, damn! What had the council 'forgotten' to tell him now?

"When this is over I will do all I can to sit and listen, I am just hoping it's not another surprise the council forgot to tell me." Alan growled.

"Oh dear!" Hopix said, "No it's nothing like that but I am afraid that it might mean the end of our partnership."

Alan had a panicked look for a second; he didn't think he could go without Hopix again. The last time had seemed like an eternity, and though he didn't want to admit it he was actually starting to feel something for her; now that she was feeling healthier, she appeared to look even more beautiful to Alan. Sighing he knew though that it would never work there sizes alone were the one deciding factor against anything happening between them, I guess it was just better not to say anything and be near her than to speak up and seem a damn fool. Sighing that was the problem though he already felt a fool just having feelings for her.

Shaking his head, he'd eliminated another of the bad guys, walking to the hill where the lizard guy was he slowly approached, expecting to see the lizard fried. Coming around, he stopped short, crap the idiot got away again! Good god what was it going to kill this ass? This was the third time he'd gotten away. Sighing he informed Hopix who was upset herself, she didn't exactly feel safe with that maniac out there hunting them.

Reaching out Alan felt everywhere; apparently, the lizard guy had run. Alan couldn't feel him anywhere on the planet. Figures Alan thought, I had thought he was a coward when I first met him now I'm sure of it. 'Oh well, ' Alan thought, as he turned toward the place where he felt the last bad Mage. 'Hmmm, ' Alan thought, 'this one isn't going to be a pushover, feels like he's been here for quite a while.'

"This last one is going to be a fight Hopix," Alan told her.

"I thought all of them were a fight for you," Hopix replied.

"In a small way, they were, but this one has an amount of power I haven't felt before, hell I haven't really felt them compared to this. I know that if I am not ready when I go into this I am a dead man." Alan said looking back at Hopix who had stopped her mouth hanging open.

"Alan you can't talk like that," Hopix told him.

"I'm sorry Hopix but it's the truth I have to be

ready, I don't think he'll try to retake the planet, or I feel that he'd already have tried. No I think he's waiting for me, hell I think a great many are waiting on me." Alan said.

"What do you mean Alan? A great many are waiting on you?" Hopix asked.

"You've noticed that no one else has shown up to try and retake the planet?" Alan asked her, to which she only nodded. "I think that a great many are waiting to see if I survive this, especially the dark council." Looking behind him, Alan looked at the empty space. "Are you really that desperate that you are actually here watching?" Alan asked.

Hopix was staring at Alan first, then the empty space; what was he doing, and whom was he talking to?

"We see, so you have gained far more knowledge than we at first thought," the red skinned leader of the dark council said.

"Yes, Reficul, I know far more than any of you realize, Alucard, Htaed, Lycaon Noacyl, should I go on?" All the members of the council he called out, each in turn gasp. "I know all of you though I find it strange that you all have human names, I also know what saying your name forward will do. Shall we try?"

"NO!" the leader roared. "You have made your point; there will be no interference from us in any regard."

"And," Alan stated.

"Nor any of our agents that haven't been here." the leader said.

"No, how about we make it, by none of your

agent's period, including lizard guy, when I destroy the last one, this planet is free from you, is that understood?" Alan told them.

"I think you go a little far," a dark human looking man with fangs said.

"No I don't Alucard, or should I say Drac... ," Alan started.

"NO!" the leader and the dark man shouted. Growling at Alan and conferring with the other 11, the leader finally spoke up.

"Alright you have your conditions, but you know we will consume you when you lose so we're not that worried. Ydnar isn't a weak child as the others were; he is far older than you think." Leaning closer the leader continued, "We will still be watching you Alan Glanto."

With that they were gone. Alan smiled he'd almost pissed his pants, they were the foulest, most evil and vile creatures Alan had ever heard of, strange but they were all creatures of human creation.

"Alan, are you ok?" A terrified and still shaking Hopix asked. She'd been terrified when the dark council suddenly appeared, plus Alan knew they were there.

Looking Alan up and down she saw no difference but she knew that he had grown in so many ways, if only... , no! She wouldn't go there again and torture herself with thoughts like that; it was enough just to be near him. Then she remembered the words of the elder of the elder on the Trembly world. She had to tell him, he needed her more than she thought.

Alan looked at Hopix god he realized it in that second he was falling for her, it couldn't happen. Alan decided he had to harden his heart to the feelings he was feeling, though he was starting to love her there was nothing he could do about it. Hopix was still shaking when she saw Alan turn toward her. Suddenly all her fears vanished, huh?

She'd never experienced this before, Alan had a strange look in his eyes a look she couldn't recognize though it did seem familiar, and then she saw it shift to pain. Pain? Why was Alan feeling pain? Then almost as suddenly, she saw that he was pushing it down, smothering everything, the pain, the emotion, the feelings it was all gone! NO! He couldn't go into the battle like this! She had to tell him everything right now!

"Alan you can't push your emotions down, it will get you killed it is how they can take you! Please Alan you have to feel! You have to I... ," Hopix was saying when the last evil mage appeared.

"I got tired of waiting! It is finally time for you to die!"

This time the being appeared as something more normal. Alan looked at the creature in front of him, though it was 12 feet high, it appeared more like a green eyed, grey colored fur covered wolf.

"It is a shame you picked such a noble creature to disguise yourself as." Alan said a hint of sadness in his voice.

"A shame huh? Why do you say that as sadly as you did," the creature asked him.

"You disgrace the image and reputation of a noble and proud creature," Alan responded.

"Noble? Proud? You are an idiot and a lout. The wolves of earth are killing machines, ruthless murderers who kill without discretion; you are a do-gooder aren't you? Good, and here I thought I might feel bad a little killing you, but not NOW!" the wolf creature said releasing a huge blast of???? 'What the hell was it' Alan thought?

Too late Alan realized it was a cold blast that weakened his shield. Firing again the next blast ripped through Alan's shield ripping a path across his arm,

"Bah!" The wolf creature growled out, "Here I thought you might be a challenge, you're more like me, no emotion nothing, when I briefly fought you before, you were almost too much but now? You're not even worth the effort." Blasting again another shot ripped past his chest raising a small trickle of blood, driving him back to the boulders that Hopix was hiding behind.

"Alan! You can't lose you can't!" Hopix whispered to him.

I am screwed, Alan thought I've lost so much, so many if only, no but before I die I have to tell her. Thinking of Hopix his shield flared, not only blocking the blast but sending it back at the wolf hitting him in the face blinding him for a few minutes. Crawling in pain Alan finally got to Hopix.

"I am sorry Hopix, I am going to die I wasn't strong enough. I have to tell you before I die, before I never have a chance." Hopix was staring at Alan what was he talking about? "I found out weeks ago that I am in love with you but I know it can never be. Please forgive me but I had to tell you before I died."

Alan had tears in his eyes as he expected her to laugh in his face. Alan had closed his eyes he didn't want the last thing he saw was her scorn and ridicule. At least he thought she would, but when he only heard her crying he opened his eyes to see her staring at him tears falling from her eyes.

"Oh my god, you love me? I thought you only tolerated me. I thought you didn't really want me around." Hopix stated.

"No! When I thought you were gone for good, all I could think of was you, I missed you that bad." A shocked Alan said.

"Alan, I love you! I have for a while now, I left home when they wanted me to stay I HAD to be with you." An excited Hopix said. The wolf creature had finally cleared its eyes that plus the fact of them sharing exchanges of love had him wanting to puke.

Alan saw the wolf creature start to move toward him, "are you two done or do I have to vomit on you to stop?" Alan stood up not noticing that the burns on his arm were almost healed.

"We'll continue this later." Alan smiled at Hopix feeling a surge of power throughout his body strange he thought. The wolf fired several bolts at Alan; almost all bounced off 1, hitting the wolf in the leg.

"You ass! How in the hell did you boost your power like that? You've never shown power like that before!." the wolf shouted at Alan.

"I don't know and right now I really don't care all that much, all I know is that you are toast!" Alan said as he started to fire at the wolf for the first time.

"Ha! So weak!" The wolf said 'til the blast skipped through the shield nearly brushing the same leg as before. For the next hour they blasted away at each other, Alan took several hits to his legs, his arms, a few brushed his face and head. Bleeding from several places Alan could only smile, the wolf was in far worse shape also bleeding in more than a few places, both were on the ground no longer able to stand, Alan's left arm was stiff he thought it might be broken in two places.

The wolf had broken legs like Alan though all four of its legs were broken; there was a gash down the left side. There were several burns to its fur, one eye had been destroyed, and its mouth was hanging open with blood coming out of it.

"Are you ready to concede defeat?" Alan asked him, "you're almost dead, your energy is gone as is nearly your life force."

"Never! You can't defeat me! I am far stronger than you!" Firing another blast Alan was barely able to block it, sending his own blast it struck the wolf's shield near its head. The wolf was screaming as the blast started to eat away at his shield, "NO! NO! I can't be defeated!" Unable to block further, the blast hit full force exploding the wolf's head; Alan tried to move back, but could not avoid being bathed in the brains and blood.

The dark council appeared a moment later, as did the white council. "Alan Glanto we concede the defeat of our agent all conditions that were agreed upon are fulfilled, you have won for now but you will be ours!" With that, they faded. The white council, all reached out freeing all the Fairixies, healing the planet, and searching they also found Hopix's brother, though badly injured he was still alive, though they didn't know how much longer. Alan could see all the pain her brother was in.

CHAPTER 2

Never one to pass on a chance to help, Alan reached out to Hopix's brother Torax, sending the absolute last of his energy he brought Torax back from the brink of death. Finally able to breathe easier, Torax opened his eyes, seeing Hopix.

Coughing, he told her, "He has to stop he is using his life force he will die, this I cannot let happen."

Afraid Hopix went to Alan, "Alan my love you have to stop, if you die I will also,"

Alan halted what he was doing. "You'll die? Why?" He asked.

"You are my life Alan Glanto; without you there can be no life, please my love rest. As you said we'll continue this later, now rest and heal." Hopix said.

Alan nodded letting the blessed darkness take him, god I'm tired he thought as he felt Hopix kiss him, 'mmm that was nice' he thought.

Hopix looked at her brother he was weak but somehow Alan had brought him back now they both needed rest, though for her brother she could heal him, at least most of the outer injuries. The more internal ones Alan would have to do, though his energy had done a partial healing as it was now her brother was alive but twisted as the children that Alan had healed had been. Standing over her brother, she had to concentrate it was hard to heal her brother when all her thoughts were on Alan.

"My god," Torax said, "after all this time it has finally happened, you are in love with the greatest Mazey that has ever been. I never thought I'd live to see the day that you would find love."

"I know," Hopix, said she could feel her brother's eyes staring at her studying her, "I couldn't believe it myself when I realized it. Before you ask, I told him he thought he was dying during the battle and told me he loved me! I thought my heart was going to burst!"

"Ok, Ok! I get it, wait, he told you he loved you? Did you tell him that you loved him?" Torax asked afraid of what she might say.

"Of course!" Hopix told her brother what did he take her for?

"How did he take the news? About the secret?" Torax said.

Here Hopix looked down, "I ... I didn't get a chance to tell him, he said we'd discuss this later." She told her brother.

"Hopix! You have to tell him, you have to! It's the law the only thing saving you right now is that he is unconscious, the minute he wakes up you have to tell him!" Torax told her a little worried; he could see the effects already starting to set in. Her wings were growing more solid, her skin was paler than it was.

"You think I don't know that? You think I want to die? I have known the results of love upon our people when it's with an outsider race." Hopix told him that though she knew he was right, the only thing saving her right now was that he was so weak and deeply unconscious.

"You have to contact mother Hopix, she's the only one that might be strong enough to heal him, and even then I'm not sure even she could do that much. Can you call her? I would but I haven't the strength." Torax said.

"I can try, it has been a very long time since I attempted this." Hopix told him.

Concentrating Hopix searched for her mother, finally finding her after a few minutes. "Mother, Mother?"

"Hopix, it has been a long time since you called me... , what's wrong? Is Alan alright?" Her mother asked.

"No mother he was hurt badly freeing the sister planet, I can no longer heal him plus he used part of his life force to bring Torax back." Hopix said.

"I will be there in a few skees, what... , what else is wrong? Something has changed, and you feel different," her mother asked.

"I am in love with Alan as he is me. Yes, I told him as he did me, but I wasn't able to tell him the secret. I am afraid I will die before I can tell him." Hopix sadly said.

"It's alright," a voice behind her, said, "momma is here."

Alan was dreaming a strange dream. He and Hopix were walking down the isle of the palace up to Queen Glimmer. Hopix was beautiful. Over and over, he heard her telling him that she loved him.

They had just reached Glimmer when the lizard guy jumped out of the crowd cutting Hopix's throat. Alan was screaming as the lizard laughed and ran out the door with no one touching him. NO!!

Alan started to go after him, but he had to heal Hopix before it was too... "I love you," Hopix choked out, "I will always love you." Then she stopped moving and breathing. Alan poured all his magic into her, but she was gone. NO! NO! NO!

Hopix's mother was having an extremely hard time with Alan. Not only was he resisting, but she felt him start to slip away on his own. Then she saw the dream, oh dear! Hopix was dead in his arms while the Queen and all her subjects were celebrating; no wonder he was slipping away.

Calling out to him, he turned, "Who the hell are you? Another come to torture me? To make me watch again and again how I failed her? To make me watch her die OVER AND OVER!?? Come, you want my life. Here it is cause without her, there is no life, you understand? Kill me slow, fast, I don't care."

"No, Alan. None of this is real. You were hurt and are healing. Hopix is here with me. She is extremely worried about you."

"I know you, but I can't place you. Who are you? How do you know these things?" Alan asked.

"I am Hopix's mother. I am here to help you, but you have to let me. You have to stop fighting me. Hopix is alive. Come with me and see." She said, taking his hand.

Snatching his hand away, he said, "Look lady, I don't really know you. You could be anyone."

"You are right; then, how about this? You reach

out outside this place and see if I am right. If Hopix isn't worried about you, I will sit here and do nothing." She said as she sat and waited. At least now he was no longer slipping away but still weak.

Reaching out, Alan had a hard time piercing outside of the Queen's palace. Another push and he was out above a blanket that was on the ground, a little higher he saw a Fairixie woman bending over him. Strange, but she had no face. Huh? Next to her, Hopix was sitting her small hand trying to hold his huge one.

Her face was covered with tears she seemed weak pale, "I have to tell you the secret of my people, what you see is an illusion. We are really..." At that moment, he was ripped away back into his body.

Alan appeared next to the woman claiming to be Hopix's mother. "Did you learn anything?" the woman asked.

"Hopix ... Hopix started to tell me something. She said her people had a secret: what I saw was an illusion." Sighing, Alan looked at the woman. "Then I was ripped away. I'm unsure what this illusion is or what you look like, but it seemed very important to her. I will try to come back. I have so little strength left."

"I will help you, when you see me again grab hold of anything I give you as tightly as you can. It is the only way I can see that you can survive." Alan nodded as she left.

Outside of his mind, Hopix's mother looked at her. She was looking better, but she wasn't saved yet. Neither was Alan. She prayed that she had the power to help him. Starting slowly, she began to infuse energy into Alan. Inside, Alan was grabbing all the energy that she sent. Almost an hour later, she had to stop. Alan wasn't as weak but was still very weak. Hopix's mother shook her head as she'd tried for an hour. Alan needed so much energy. She could feel he was almost out of danger, but there was a risk.

She needed to rest, but all of Hopix's people on both planets owed Alan so much. If only ... She hadn't heard of it being done since before she was born, well over ten thousand years ago. She had to try. She felt it was the only thing that could save him.

Standing she called to all the Fairixies on the planet... [The Mezey Alan was hurt very badly defeating the evil ones. I am the strongest healer from the home planet. I ask you to lend me a small piece of your selves to help heal him. My thanks to those that do, but no one will look down on those too afraid. I understand.]

Waiting a few minutes, she felt energy begin to trickle in. She placed her hand on Alan. She'd been at it for ten minutes when an almost overwhelming flood of energy suddenly hit and passed through her into Alan. Alan's body jerked as the energy hit him. Smiling, the woman could feel him suddenly grow stronger.

Most of the internal injuries were healed now. An hour later, a little light headed woman smiled at Hopix. "He will be alright now. Everything inside is good though I am afraid he will have to do the outside. He only heard part of the secret. He needs to hear the rest. You have maybe an hour after he wakes. No more. Do not delay, daughter. Bring your brother home." With that, the woman pulled a cube a lot like Alan's out and was gone.

Has Mother been to the Trembly world? When, Hopix wondered. Had she been a helper like Hopix? Smiling, that could explain a lot of things. Was her Father human like Alan?

White mages lived a long time almost as long as the Fairixies did. Strange, she thought. She never remembered seeing a human when she was little. Mulling it over, she decided she'd look into it later. First, she needed to save Alan and then herself.

As she watched, Hopix could finally see Alan start to breathe a lot easier. She just hoped her mother had been able to save him. After what he'd told her, she felt that she couldn't go on without him. Then, as an afterthought, she knew she couldn't survive. It was part of the secret and the main reason Hopix hadn't found love in such a long time.

Alan's dreams had drastically changed. Over and over, he kept reliving the lizard guy getting away. Everything he tried got him hurt or almost killed. Each time, Alan could himself as he got increasingly angry.

Hopix could feel the bad dreams that Alan was having. Strange, she thought. After what mother had done, he shouldn't have bad dreams. Reaching in but not too far because her power was weaker, she saw that Alan was dreaming about the lizard guy again. Then she felt the tether that the lizard guy was attached to, that was it! Pulling out, she grabbed Alan's head, concentrating as hard as she could. She knew this could kill her because she was too weak to do this full power. Shaking her head, she knew this could exhaust all her power, but for Alan she'd gladly give her life.

The lizard guy was getting away again when Alan turned and saw Hopix was there. Shocked for a moment, and then he thought it was another trick. That is 'til he saw how weak and pale she was. "Alan," she gasped out, "it's all a fake it's the lizard guy cut his tether look at him you'll..." Hopix groaned. "It will end all his interference. Hurry, my love. I wait for you," she said as she fell, then faded.

Now even madder than before, Alan walked up to the lizard guy. "It's over, you ass!"

Cutting the tether, he heard the lizard guy scream. "Next time we meet, the first thing I will take will be your ability to move. Then your council can have you!"

Lizard guy smirked, "As if. You not only don't have enough power, but you won't kill."

Alan tried to follow it out as soon as the creep was gone. The closer to the top he got, the harder it was. Finally opening his eyes, he tried to sit up. No dice too damn weak. Looking around, he saw Hopix lying in a crumpled heap. NO! He crawled the two feet to her with every bit of his strength. Touching her, he could feel that she was extremely weak. Though he didn't have much energy, he had to save her.

Though there was really no future for them, he had to try. With tears falling from his eyes, he held his hand over her chest. At first, there was nothing. Alan started to swear and then pushed harder. Finally, he could feel the energy start to slowly flow from him. She was so weak. He had to save her. There was nothing that he wouldn't do for her, including dying as he was prepared to save her.

Alan had already tapped his life force a few moments later, when her eyes fluttered open. "NO ALAN," she tried to shout. "Let me go. I did everything for you." Now, she was gasping as she could feel her failing body start to strengthen.

"I have to, Hopix. I love you, and I'd gladly give my life for you," Alan said. Hopix felt a huge jump in her life force.

"I love you Alan, but you have to understand. Once we are committed to each other there will be no other. Our lives will literally be entwined, dependent upon each other, to live." Hopix said starting to feel better already.

"This was all the secret of your people?" Alan asked, he'd actually stopped feeling Hopix's energy growing.

"Well its part of it." Here, she giggled. Sitting up, Hopix's body was suddenly outlined with light. Alan's mouth hung open as Hopix's body started to grow. ALL of her body started to grow. Finally after possibly five minutes, Hopix stood. Alan's mouth hung open. My god, she was gorgeous! He'd thought before that for a light green skinned being with wings, she was kind of sexy! Holy shit, Alan thought. Here I am on death's doorway and I'm getting horny over a, looking back at Hopix, he thought sexy as hell woman with wings!

Hopix's mouth hung open, "you really think I am sexy?" Alan could swear that Hopix was blushing like a virgin ... It was then that he remembered that Hopix had said that she hadn't been home in thousands of years. Alan guessed he had a shocked look on his face since Hopix was giggling like a little girl.

Alan just shook his head; a virgin at her age? Hopix looked at him shyly, "Yes, Alan. I am a v ... one of those. I started working for the council a long time ago."

"You've never met anyone you wanted to be with?" Alan asked. At the vigorous shaking of her head, Alan was a little shocked. As sexy as she was, and no one had wanted her?

What the hell? Were all the idiots she'd met blind as hell? Again, this started Hopix giggling. Then she realized that Alan wasn't kidding. Looking at herself, she didn't see anything special. She had 34C breasts, weighed one hundred eighty pounds, light green eyes and skin, and was a little shorter than Alan's six foot two inches standing six feet. The fact that her stomach was flat and her hips were slender didn't register with her, as Alan was staring at those parts intensely.

"Alan, why are you staring at me? I am the same Hopix you met that first day," she said, a little embarrassed that Alan couldn't take his eyes off her; truly a first for her. Well, it was a first 'til Alan started to feel weak again and had to lie back down as his head started to swim.

She rushed to his side. Alan had been trying to bring his energy up the whole time he and Hopix had been talking. Closing his eyes and laying his head in Hopix's lap, he felt his power was so low. Trying to reach out, he started bringing in what little power he felt slowly at first and then bit by bit faster.

Finally, an hour later, he sat up. Looking around, he saw all the destruction that he and the last bad mage had caused.

I have to fix this, he thought. The only problem was when he sat up, he noticed that one arm and both legs were practically useless right now. That, plus the amount of pain he was in didn't help either. Finally situated, he started slowly on both legs. Almost an hour later he had finished. Whew, Alan thought. That helped quite a bit. At least now I can concentrate more. He was about to start on his arms when he saw Hopix's brother Torax.

Walking to him, Torax was amazed that Alan's legs were working. "I made a promise to Hopix that I'd bring you back safe. Right now, I am failing at that. I can see the pain you are in." With that, Alan started first on Torax's back. 10 minutes later, Torax was amazed that the pain was gone. "I need to finish the rest of your insides. I got you out of danger, but I can feel 1 of your lungs starting to fail. I'm not sure if the other three can keep you going as bruised as they are."

Torax could only nod, his mouth hanging open. Another twenty minutes and Alan pronounced him as good as Alan could get him. Alan knew he had to hurry. True, he'd regained a lot of strength, but there was still pain masking a lot of his power. Leaning over Torax one more time, Alan started in extremely slow, trying to give his body a chance to recharge some. Again, Torax's mouth hung open when he felt the pain in both legs fade and he could move them!

Finally done as much as he could do, Alan had to sit. Hopix held him as he lay down. Torax was amazed. His big sister was beautiful! He wasted no time at all walking to her on shaky legs (he hadn't been able to walk for over a year now) and letting her know how proud he was of her. It was then that his concern for Alan surfaced.

"Why is he so weak Hopix? Didn't mother heal him?" He asked.

"Yes she did, but..." Hopix lightly brushed a now sleeping Alan's hair from his face. "Alan is very strong, even as strong as mother is. It took all she had plus some from the others here for her to heal his insides. After that he had surpassed even her. Then, when he awoke he'd just finished his legs when he said he saw you. He said he could see the pain you were in."

"Yes, he told me that he had promised you to bring me back safe, that he was failing in that task" Torax said.

Hopix was in shock he let his own healing go to fulfill a promise he made to her? Looking at the man on her lap she could swear that she fell in love with him more at that moment. "I am going to try and do what I can," Hopix said as she reached over and concentrated on her brother's arms.

Hopix had been working on her brother for almost two hours when she felt his left arm start to straighten.

Another hour and she felt it slip where it should be, the right was far worse and would require a lot more than she had, but at least almost all the pain was gone.

Almost falling, her brother caught her with his good arm. This in itself amazed him, and laid her next to Alan. Covering them both, he tried to fly but found the pain in his right shoulder wouldn't let him off the ground far. Concentrating, he sought the nearest Fairixies, asking them if they could bring food to them. Agreeing soon at least twenty Fairixies showed up bowing to Alan and Torax.

Torax moved closer to them, explaining a few things that had them all nodding. They were staring at him, the fact that both legs were working and one arm. Torax explained that the Mezey had healed him at risk to its own life. All twenty of the Fairixies mouths were hanging open. Torax went on to tell them that NO one was to say anything when they appeared the next day. They all agreed and promised to spread the word.

Back on the Fairixie's home world Hopix's mother was staring at the cube. It was good to see her sontaking an active role in his rescue. Finally, she thought. Hopix had finally found love. Now she would have her full power. Smiling, she remembered her love. One day, she thought, one day. They would find a way to free you. Darling, she thought, how I have missed you. The nights are so lonely without you.

She was glad he had left his seed so she could have more children in case he disappeared, though she hated that none of her children knew their father. A fine man, the last good human 'til Alan. Finally, the balance was shifting back again. It would be soon. Alan had the cube, if any could, it was him.

The next morning, Alan jerked awake unsure of where he was, plus the fact that a soft pair of breasts were pressed into his back. Alan knew it wasn't his wife. Hell, that bitch screamed if he looked at them, let alone touched them. Turning over, his eyes opened wide as a pair of beautiful light green eyes met them. Being a man, he looked lower seeing as near to perfect a set of breasts as he'd seen in a very long time. Hopix's eyes opened wide. Looking down, she stared at her breasts. Huh? She thought, perfect? What did he mean by that they were just breasts though they had felt so good pressed into Alan's back?

Looking further under the cover, he started to choke. She was stark naked! OMG! Again he could only stare. She was, for lack of a better word, perfect to him. At that moment, he realized that he loved her more if possible. Hopix sat up in shock he really did love her that much. She thought that she'd dreamed that part. Alan watched as her clothes crawled up her body, and she was dressed in seconds.

"I am sorry, Alan. I forgot to tell you that I sleep in the raw. I have for a thousand years. I apologize, but from what I heard, you seemed to enjoy it." She giggled again.

"I hope to show you one day just how much I love you, Hopix." Alan had to adjust his tented pants in front of him.

"Alan, if you are in pain, I can help you," Hopix smiled sweetly, leaning low in front of Alan looking at his pants and Alan down her shirt.

"NO, I don't think so Hopix. We don't have that much time. Believe me; I would need quite a bit of time." Alan said. Taking a shivering breath, he tried to calm his overactive hormones. Hopix looked at

Alan wondering what he was talking about. Though the more she thought about the tent in Alan's pants the more excited she got. That's odd, she thought. I've been around Alan for weeks; this is the first time I've gotten these feelings. Alan and her brother looked at each other and smiled. They could see that she was going to be thinking about this for the rest of the day. Alan looked at Torax's arms, surprised when he found the left almost completely healed.

Looking back at Hopix, Alan looked at Torax. "Last night, while you were asleep on her lap, she tried to do both of them, but she said the right was very bad." Torax said.

"Alright this will hurt for a few seconds. I am feeling an old break that didn't heal right, so it will re-break then heal." Alan explained to Torax. Torax gritted his teeth before Alan started. There were two sickening snaps of bone and then Alan was pouring energy into the arm. Fifteen minutes later the arm was like new as was the other.

Sitting down Alan had to concentrate on his half good arm first. It took almost half an hour. As soon as it was one hundred percent, Alan felt his concentration and power jump. Starting in on his other arm, he was half done when his stomach roared. Oh crap, Alan thought. I haven't eaten in over twenty four hours. Stopping, he made a table and chairs appear. On the table was food for him, with a few things he knew that Hopix and her brother had been yearning for. Finishing, Alan felt his power jump more. He then started on his arm again.

Another thirty minutes, and he was done.

Looking around, Alan had to fix this, the sheer destruction he and the last mage had caused. Concentrating, Alan could see how the planet was supposed to be. True, the council had fixed most of the big things but a few little things were just as important. Reaching out Alan first repaired all the damage where they were, then further out he came to the first city, all over the planet he went. The council had done an extremely good job. Finally finished, Alan opened his mind to speak to the whole planet.

[Good people, the days of slavery and death are over. I will be leaving for the home world shortly. Any that wish to go back, I will be here for one more of your time units. If any wish to go back, be here before then. I will let you decide. Be well all.]

With that Alan sat and ate a little more. He needed to keep his strength up for this trip in case a lot wished to return. Not long after he'd spoken he estimated that about 100 showed up.

"Alright, I want everyone to hold hands and do not let go, although this won't take long." They had lined up when Hopix pulled her cube out, smiling at Alan. He could only shake his head and smile back at her.

They were about to go when they heard a voice. "Thank you, it is a long journey from the other side of the planet," said a young looking mother holding a baby. Alan smiled. He was glad she made it; to be able to start over on the home planet was a blessing in deed. They had flashed out when the lizard creature appeared.

He'd been trying to control every Fairixie he saw

but like before they were sealed against mind controlling powers; now, that's alright he knew where they were going. Laughing he knew that Alan and the Fairixie were going to get married. He would kill her in the palace and then get Alan later while he was depressed for being a failure. Laughing evilly, the lizard guy flashed out.

Alan, Hopix and the rest of the Fairixies appeared not far from the palace, several guards bristled 'til they saw Alan then they stood at attention. All the new arrivals were staring with their mouths agape at all of the buildings here on the Fairixie home world. Alan still felt a little unsure; the dream with the lizard guy had seemed all too real to just be a dream. They were soon greeted by many more servants and guards; looking around, Alan saw Glimmer approaching them.

"I want all of you to meet Queen Glimmer she rules here," Alan told them.

They all bowed, again their mouths a gape at the splendor and beauty of the queen. Glimmer looked at Alan closely then at Hopix, "Finally!" She said, throwing her hands up. "I thought you two would never get together! Everyone could see it but you two."

Alan looked at her strangely, "How pray tell can you tell?"

"It's obvious; she has told you the secret of us, Alan I can tell you are still having trouble seeing the truth. Look in your heart and think of your love for Hopix with your eyes closed. Then I want you to open them." Glimmer said with crossed arms.

Doing as she asked, he slowly opened his eyes,

Holy shit! Alan backed up a few steps, everything; almost everyone was close to the size he was! What the hell was going on here? They could hear Hopix giggle as Alan backed away from her and Queen Glimmer. "Serves you right still having doubts after watching me grow," Hopix said.

"Hey! If you were in my position, you'd be having doubts yourself! Besides, I didn't think you would be this beautiful when I got a really good look at you!" Alan said, starting to get a little annoyed. Looking around further, it was almost as if his eyes were different, the colors were sharper, and everything he looked at seemed one hundred times better than he'd remembered them.

"There," Glimmer said seeing Alan's reaction, "everything seems far clearer now doesn't it? I mean with your vision of course," Glimmer added with a smile.

Looking around, he saw that everything was far more colorful than he at first thought, plus his real, first good look at Glimmer, had almost taken his breath away. Shaking his head he had to admit she was gorgeous, that is 'til he turned and saw Hopix, his mouth dropped open he wasn't able to catch his breath.

Staring at her he couldn't believe his eyes! She was by far more beautiful than he could put into words, if he could speak at the moment that is. Her light green eyes were flashing in pride and love toward him, usually, he'd have been uncomfortable, but right now he could only feel the warmth of her love. Oh my god! He thought she didn't even realize how perfect she was to me!

Hopix could hear all his thoughts, she was perfect to him? What did he mean by that? She was the same old Hopix that she'd always been. Looking at her body she saw that her nipples were hard from his staring at them, pressing against the material of her dress. What was going on? Why was she feeling so warm under his gaze? She'd have to ask her mother later, she had to remember to speak to her. Shaking her head she also noticed that Alan was uncomfortable again, it seemed his pants were causing him problems again.

"Alan, if you are in as much pain as it appears; you should let me help you with it!" Hopix told him.

Alan turned away from Glimmer and Hopix trying to adjust his self before things got out of hand. Glimmer could only shake her head, her own husband had been as bad when she first met him, but unlike Hopix she wasn't a virgin. Again shaking her head at the predicament, she really needed to take Hopix aside and advise her of a few things. Suddenly Glimmer realized that she might be a grandmother soon, this caused an even bigger smile to break out on her face.

Hopix noticed and walked to her, "Queen Glimmer are you alright? I just noticed you were smiling strangely."

"Oh, I am fine my dear but I think we need to have a short talk," Hopix nodded looking at her and then Alan people were acting so strange lately, as was her body. Alan watched as Hopix and Glimmer went to the other side of the room, still uncomfortable; Alan just stood there undecided about what to do, that is 'til Torax flew next to him.

"So you both have finally realized that you love each other well for you it is far more simple, but I take it you have guessed that Hopix is a virgin?" Torax said.

"Yes," Alan replied as he watched Hopix's face start to blush scarlet; what was causing that, he thought? "I realized it not too long ago."

"My sister is older than me, but I have an advantage over her in many ways, she has never been in love. As I have heard it put by the council, she blamed herself for many of the mage failures that have happened over the last few thousand years. She has worked tirelessly to try and correct what she felt were her mistakes." Torax related to him.

"Her mistakes? How are they her mistakes? How the mage she trains uses their power is in no way her fault." Alan told Torax.

Here Torax smirked, "You know my sister, she took the entire universe on her shoulders trying to bring the balance back to it."

"Yes, I know very well, you mean to tell me she hasn't stopped in thousands of years 'til she found me?" Alan asked Torax, his mouth hanging open.

Torax's smile grew, "You've just about got it, I am proud that you have finally got her to open her heart, it will be a wonderful change from the all business sister I have had the last few thousand years. Just remember, Alan my soon to be brother in law, be gentle with her she is most definitely delicate and fragile, I am afraid that her heart and emotions would never recover if they are broken. Oh, I forgot; her mother might not react all that good either." Torax snickered as he walked away.

Damn, he was on dangerous ground but then again it shouldn't be; he did love Hopix he owed her more than just his life and love. Looking over at Hopix and Queen Glimmer he could see that Hopix's mouth was hanging open and the scarlet color on her face was still there.

Walking over he heard them both quiet suddenly, "Hopix I have to contact the council and let them know what is going on." Hopix stared at him her mouth still hanging open, and could only nod.

Shaking his head Alan walked outside and called the council. "Ah! Good Alan you have done an exceedingly good job; the balance has finally started to shift in a more positive direction. We wish to give our congratulations on your upcoming wedding to Hopix." They told him.

"Wait, wait, wait, my upcoming wedding?" His skin started to glow as did his eyes, "I haven't said or thought anything about a wedding to Hopix, I haven't even thought of asking her yet!" Alan shouted, blowing half the council off their seats, shattering several windows in the palace, and blowing a certain lizard man into view.

"So you son of a bitch you found me after all!" The lizard man shouted though Alan could see that he was shaking. Reaching out Alan brutally smashed through his defenses and started to snap his powers. Screaming the lizard man flashed out, though unknown to Alan he couldn't leave the Fairixie's planet for a while. Turning back to the now shielded council Alan's power started to flare higher now, Alan was about to crush the shields of the council when a soft sweet voice spoke.

"Alan my love? Come to me my love, please don't hurt them." Hopix stood in front of several huddled and terrified Fairixies at the entrance to the palace. Turning Alan saw a scared and shaking Hopix staring at him wide eyed she'd never seen his power flare this high or this violently. Almost immediately, Alan felt ashamed, all his life he'd felt this fear at one point or another like Hopix and her people were feeling, watching him. Hanging his head Alan reached in his pocket and pulled the cube from it.

Hopix's eyes grew large when she saw what Alan was about to do, "NO ALAN! PLEASE, NO!" Hopix begged of Alan as she flew toward him. Sadly he looked up at her then, and without ceremony Alan vanished.

Hopix was suddenly angry, turning she didn't see that her power had more than doubled. Looking at the council, she gritted her teeth, "If I have lost him, the council will pay! I just found the one being in the universe who completes me, and you drove him to this. I guarantee that if he can't be found, there will be retribution from the Fairixie people! You all know who I am, though you will soon find out what I can do!" Palming her cube, Hopix also vanished.

Queen Glimmer smirked, she'd wanted Hopix to express more emotion as her mother did, but this was a little beyond what both of them had wanted. Smiling to herself, she looked at the small screen in her hand; thank goodness she'd planted that homing button on him the last time he was here. Reaching out, she felt Hopix heading to earth shaking her head she thought Hopix would learn soon, home was the last place Alan would go. Especially with that terror of a female that he'd been mated to living there. As she could see Alan was going in the opposite direction, ah! So he was going to see friends after all, good thing they were hers as well.

Alan appeared on the Trembly world for the second time shielding himself he didn't want the Trembly to feel him. He especially didn't want them to feel the deep depression that he was feeling, he'd terrified the first person being that truly loved him. It was a feeling that had warmed him deeply, lightening his soul and making him feel better than he'd ever felt. He'd seen her shaking, and the terror on her people's faces, he knew then in that moment he was no better than the evil that he'd defeated.

Then again he wondered why he'd chosen this planet to come to, all they would do here would try and convince him that he wasn't evil and try to get him to go back. After what he'd done he wasn't all too sure he could ever go back. Sighing, well, this was starting out real good just a minute of thinking, and he was already twice as far down in his depression as he was when he arrived.

He'd been there maybe an hour when he felt a stirring, not much at first, but it was there, shit Alan thought they found me I hadn't done anything to attract them. Waiting Alan knew they would be there soon no matter what he did, they would find him so he sat still and waited.

Within minutes, the leader he'd met before was floating far from him. "Hail Tranzarie it is good to see you again though we would like to actually see you. Please forgive me for not getting close, but you are so full of low energy and emotions I am afraid I cannot come too close."

Smirking a half smile, Alan thought if they only knew that what they wished was actually here and it was poisonous to them.

"I will not ask why you are here but it appears that you are where you need to be. May I hear what has transpired since you last blessed us with life that was fleeing the planet?" Sighing Alan wasn't really in a mood to talk but didn't have much choice as he was only a guest here.

Alan started slowly at first, describing the many battles of the evil ones of the sister planet of Queen Glimmer and Hopix's planet. He told of how he was hurt and healed by the love he had found and then the anger he'd felt, the abject terror he'd seen on the faces of Hopix's people, and the fear on her face.

The whole time Alan watched the leader; he neither accused, objected, nor said a word. Alan was starting to feel a little better just what he'd been afraid of when he first landed here, but it was the one place he felt no one would look for him in. Suddenly Alan stopped feeling a presence behind him, looking he saw literally thousands of the green fuzzy life forms behind him. Oh great he thought, they weren't looking all that great.

"Why do they all look so sick?" Alan asked the leader.

"They are sick because you helped them so much before and now they cannot repay you when you are in such need. It has saddened them so badly that they are now sick with the pain." The leader explained. Oh great, I thought I could hide here and am killing all these gentle, peace-loving creatures. If he wasn't feeling bad before he really was now. "Leader/Elder I am going, I almost killed many who are dear to me now my mere presence is killing your people. I only hope that the next place I go that the death I meet there is horrible and as painful as the pain I am causing you and them."

As Alan rose, the leader stopped him, "Great Tranzarie please before you leave, can you feel inside and tell us who it is controlling you?"

Shocked a moment, Alan looked within and saw that there was a strong magical hand of magic on him a very familiar hand.

Growling Alan called the light council, "I need all of you to witness this." Alan told them. "Reficul! I know you are watching I can feel you and your magic in me you made a vow that you would keep out of what I did directly." With a flourish, the Dark Council appeared all of the 12 growlings at Alan, Taking the magic presence and making it clear to all. Alan looked accusingly at the council especially the red skinned leader.

"You broke a magical vow therefore I invoke ... your name LUCIFER!" Alan shouted the red skinned leader screamed as his skin started to flay off the body being replaced and reflayed again and again.

"I also know he wasn't the only one Dracula! Death! Was he?" The other two members started to scream as they were also were flayed over and over. "One of the conditions of winning the fight with the tenth mage on the sister planet you yourself, Reficul said, 'there will be no interference from us in any regard.' You have broken this; therefore, I call for the continued judgment upon the entire council. If you or your agents break this again, the judgment will enact."

"You cannot call for that!" A pale member of the dark council called.

"No, he cannot, though it is his right to ask us to, under the circumstances it will be enacted. An agent can only act out against Alan if he is on a world controlled by the dark council. Then only to try and keep the planet, I am afraid Alan it is on you and we may only step in when something is wrong or you win the world. Realize that everything changes now, you no longer will have us to help you while you are there and are at the mercy of the agent there." the leader of the light council warned Alan. "Many out there are stronger than the last you faced on the sister world."

Smiling a huge smile, Alan nodded, "I accept, the dark council needs to realize I am no longer the unknowing earth man I was, I have gained far more than they might think I have, much more," this last almost whispered as Alan looked at the light council and smiled.

Alan turned and saw that the Tremblys were hiding not far away, hiding in a great many flowers that he hadn't seen before. Bending to the ground he placed a hand over them and could feel Hopix, all her love, all her patience all of her. Smiling, he finally knew what he had to do; bowing to the council he invited them to the wedding when Hopix and her mother planned it that is if he wasn't on a mission. Looking at the dark council, he almost felt sorry for the three members being tortured by their own treachery. Thinking a moment he thought of the release words. "Relicul, Alucard, Htaed desaeler era uoy, evael I Nehw."

Passing his hand over the empty field, Alan smiled when several other types of flowers and very small trees suddenly grew. "Another thank you to you and your people for helping me find myself." Alan told the now shocked leader, he hadn't seen the small trees in a thousand years since he was small. Grasping the cube Alan smiled even larger he could feel Hopix, goodness she was worried. With a pop Alan flashed out, the three on the dark council suddenly released and dropping to the ground. All three looked at the light council with extreme hatred and malice in their eyes.

"Ha! You should have known not to go against one as smart as him. Especially when you gave him access to all the knowledge like you did!" The gnome leader of the light council said.

"Know that you and your agent will pay for this! Your agent isn't..." the dark council leader started.

"We already know what is in his heart, and we better than you know the FULL extent of his power. You do not want to experience it though you got a taste a few moments ago. Be forewarned he does have full knowledge of all the in and outs of the councils. As he has already liberated the Tremblys, he also has a source of even more information. As I said be warned, now he is far from through!" The leader of the light council said.

"He will soon see that we also are far from through, the battle is coming soon his planet will be the battleground if he continues to liberate the worlds we have rightfully claimed! Best you advise him of that!" The red skinned leader of the dark council warned. With a flourish and a dark cloud, the dark council disappeared.

Shaking his head, the light council leader needed to advise Alan before they sent him out again though Alan had tipped the balance on earth more toward the light there were still a great many dark agents there.

Alan flashed into the hotel room looking around he didn't feel Hopix anywhere he could have sworn that she was ... hmmm, it appeared they had passed each other, grasping the cube he was about to flash out when he felt a presence.

Hopix appeared in the hotel room, but there was no sign of Alan looking through the few things he had there hoping for a clue as to where he had gone. More tired than she thought she was, she laid down, a dream came to her that she should go home and wait for him there, she did, and Alan appeared a few moments later, grabbing him she kissed him a hot and passionate kiss that could melt the strongest metal. As she started to feel faint from the amount of love that he put into the kiss, the lizard guy appeared lunging forward to drive a knife into her back.

Alan turned her at the last instant taking the knife in his side. Screaming, her eyes and body glowing Hopix's power rose to monstrous levels reaching she grabbed the lizard guy who laughed and waved his hand. Hopix started to laugh when nothing happened.

"You pathetic little man!" Hopix's voice echoed off the walls of the palace and every other building nearby, "You no longer realize that you are dead!" With that Hopix's power climbed higher as the lizard guy's skin began to melt, his eyes popping out like loose marbles. An eerie scream issued from his throat 'til it turned to a gurgling death rattle. Smiling Hopix watched as the last of the lizard guy melted to a mass of putrid wetness on the ground.

Jerking awake Hopix was shaking, the dream had been so real, still shaking she grasped the cube, she had to go home and talk to her mother, the Queen wouldn't do this time; it had to be her mother. Flashing out she was only gone a moment when Alan flashed in, looking around he was about to go when he felt her, reaching out he had her appear in front of him.

"Now then, you cannot leave you are cut off from your body, mostly, tell me your mission and I'll let you go." Alan told her.

When she spit on him Alan smiled a wicked smile that for a moment scared her, and then she laughed 'til she felt her energy starting to fade. "How about it? I can leave you here in a rotting corpse, when it dies so do you then you are the dark council's and you know how forgiving they are. Besides according to you, I am powerless to stop anything you do."

The woman started to tell all, squeezing harder, including the lizard guy's plans. Alan made a scissors motion above her then she was gone, as was the body. Hmmm, so lizard guy thought he could kill them; smiling, Alan thought, well he has another thing coming.

CHAPTER 3

Alan appeared not far from the Queen's palace reaching out he started to search for Hopix. Ah! There she was safe and ... not all that sound after the dream, but Alan would soon fix that. Reaching out again, he began to search for the Lizard guy; shaking his head Alan thought this guy really had lost his mind to go against Alan who obviously had far superior power than his? Alan decided that this needed to end once and for all, though he didn't kill unless he had no choice this was the one time that Alan had no regrets about ending another beings life.

Alan had gone over almost all the planet when he finally found lizard man. Flashing out he appeared next to the hiding coward, reaching out Alan grabbed the being by the throat only to watch as the man started to laugh at him.

"Ah! I see that you got to that little bitch I planted there to screw up your little whore!" This brought on a new bout of laughing from the guy. "You really thought it would be that easy? I have agents all over this pathetic dust ball! I will make everyone on this planet suffer as you made my brother and his children sud..."

Alan had enough as he started to squeeze the being tighter, prompting another round of laughter. "I really don't see what is so damn funny," Alan told him.

"Go ahead kill me if you can! You are never going to find them all in time without me!" The lizard guy started to laugh harder at Alan. "Besides you don't have the balls to..." the guy started to scream, then foam at the mouth.

Alan leaned close and appeared in the visions he'd created in the evil being's mind, "You might be right though, concerning you I have nothing to stop me from killing you, so here's how it's going to go. You get to live through all the pain you have caused, including the deaths, up to the moment of death over and over. Remember an old saying we have on earth, you'd be surprised what you can live through. Enjoy asshole; I know I will every excruciating moment. Each delicious scream you utter, you see I am far from what you are, but I still believe that you deserve the punishment that equals the crime."

With that Alan started to withdraw only to have the lizard guy scream, "You can't do this! You are good you aren't allowed!"

Alan drew up to the Lizard's guys face and snarled, "In case you missed it, I am not the goody two shoes you thought neither am I an evil bastard like you and your brother were, talk and I'll end it, refuse?" Here Alan shrugged, "All I can say is what I did before; enjoy asshole. Withdrawing Alan smiled as the screams became louder and more desperate.

The light council was waiting when his eyes opened. "Alan, do you really think that was necessary?" The leader of the council stated.

Alan turned an almost feral growl coming from his throat. "Necessary?! This son of a bitch has gone after me, he's gone after my Fairixie friends, and he's been planning the death of the woman I love! You think that this is UNNECESSARY!!! I will not stop 'til I have all of them here, unless you want to take me off being your little problem solver! If that is the case, then you can kiss my ass!"

Suddenly Alan heard a small voice, "Alan? My love, are you alright?" Immediately Alan felt all the anger leave his body. "I felt you appear then I felt your anger, please, my love let me help you." Hopix said not far away.

"My dear, you have helped me far more than you will ever know." Turning back to the council Alan informed them, "This one claims to have agents working on this world to destroy all that has been finally put right. I cannot stop 'til I know the truth. I realize that my methods are different than what you are used to but I have to know as I feel you do also."

"Your methods do not anger us we are just concerned the path you are on right now can only lead to trouble later on." Another of the council members said a look of genuine concern on her face.

This was the first time Alan had really looked at the light council, there was, of course, the gnome type creature that was the leader, but the rest were an odd combination. He was seeing what he could only describe as a brownie, a centaur, an actual imp, the Elf was no surprise, a Nymph, a Sprite, and what he can only describe as a Valkyrie (there were two of them). There appeared to be a Banshee, but the one who had just spoken to him caught his attention the most. She was a Fairixie, and had he not known better was an almost exact double to Hopix.

Alan bowed low to the council feeling the rage leaving his body again, strange but Hopix's image always had a calming effect upon him. "I apologize to the council for anything I have done to upset it, but as I said, I have to find out, I figure a few hours of torture ought to loosen his tongue." Alan told them.

Though they weren't thrilled about it, they let him continue, warning him that he was walking an extremely thin line. Alan nodded then watched as they left. Hopix flew to him a moment later a look of major concern on her face. Then she launched herself into his arms grasping him as close to her chest as she could. As tears started to fall from her eyes she weakly hit him in the chest with her fists. "I was so scared my love," she started her face still buried in his chest. "I felt for you everywhere but it was like you had disappeared! Please my love, don't leave me again; whatever is wrong we can overcome."

"I know this now Hopix, I felt what you did on the Trembly world, and you never do anything half way. You always put all you are into it. Your love is far more powerful than any power that I will ever possess, though I did not wish for you to see what I am having to do, I will not hide it from you either." Alan told her as he kissed her. The shock that went through them both amazed them as they were unable to move for a few minutes.

From a doorway not far away Hopix's mother

looked on, tears streaming from her eyes finally they had sealed the bond never again would her little girl feel alone. Now it was on Alan to nourish her soul with the love she could feel pouring out of them. Withdrawing, she knew her work was done as she faded into the shadows and was gone.

"Alan, I had such a horrible dream, the lizard guy killed you, and I lost control it felt as if all your power and mine combined as I ... I, k ... k ... killed him it was like nothing I've ever experienced." Hopix said as fresh tears of pain began to fall from her eyes.

Clutching her closer Alan rubbed her back and kissed her face, finally, after a few minutes Alan felt her relax. Oh shit! Alan thought as he suddenly felt Hopix's nipples try to bore holes into his chest; this did nothing to calm the now tenting in his pants that Hopix for the moment, was ignoring though Alan was sure she wouldn't ignore for long.

A moment later Alan realized that it wouldn't be an issue THIS time as he felt Hopix's breathing was slow and even. Wow, Alan thought, she feels that secure with me that she fell asleep on me here? Now I really know she loves me. Sighing Alan just hoped that he wasn't a disappointment to her later on.

Alan lifted Hopix into his arms and grasped the cube thinking of the palace as he didn't know where Hopix's home was. Appearing inside the throne room, Queen Glimmer looked at Alan with shock, "is she alright? Do you need a healer?" Came Glimmer's voice.

"No, I think she's just exhausted, did your men take care of the lizard guy I left there?" Alan asked.

"Yes, he's in a cell that no magic can penetrate. He actually said that there were agents here on this world?" Glimmer asked a little fearful that such treachery was still on the planet after Alan had cleared it.

Sighing Alan nodded, "I found out that this one is a rogue from the dark council, with an agenda that is all his own, from his sick twisted mind." Alan told her as he laid Hopix down on a nearby couch. "I brought her here after everything that happened. I didn't know where her home is."

"Here is fine Alan, we owe you and Hopix more than you can ever know. So you truly love her as you came back to her." The Queen suddenly stated shocking Alan a moment.

"Yes, though how you know is curious to me." Alan told her then his eyes grew wide as the Queen withdrew a cube similar to the one that he and Hopix had. "So you have visited the Tremblys also."

The Queen shook her head yes, then a veil of sadness covered her face. "Actually, my mate and I did many of your centuries ago, not too long before I conceived my first child. He was much like you Alan though not as powerful, but he had a few tricks that allowed him to get by on what he had. Not long after I conceived Glimix he left on a mission to free a world a lot like the Tribocs, the people there were even more untrusting of him. He'd just started to heal them when he was betrayed, the fact that he had helped a good many saved his life but he was rendered unconscious." Here Glimmer sighed, the story always made her soul feel heavy with the pain of loss.

Alan could feel the change in Glimmer the deep pain and suffering that she hid so very well from others laid bare in front of him. This pain feels familiar, Alan thought a longing deep pain for love that wasn't returned because it wasn't there. Oh yeah Alan knew that pain all too well the same pain he'd suffered with that bitch of a wife. Alan could feel the crippling effect it was having on her.

"I am sorry, Alan I did not mean to bother you with this; it is a pain that I bare each day." Glimmer told him the sadness starting to fade as quickly as it had appeared.

"It's alright Glimmer I too know this pain you feel though I felt it with someone that I loved but never had the loved returned. I lived with the pain a long time also, if I can get the council to agree I will find him and bring him back. I have to make sure this world is clear first. I can't have Hopix and all my friends here in danger now can I?" Alan's smile surprised the Queen as she felt one start across her lips, a true smile that she hadn't worn in a very long time.

"You have done far more than I can ever thank you for, you have returned the Princess Glimix to me, you have restored our world, and healed so many that were beyond the help of the healers. You have restored almost all the cities to their former glory, you have freed the sister world and opened a way to them now. You do realize that we can never repay you fully?" The Queen said a look of true gratitude on her face.

"Now you wish to help return my mate to me? He left his seed for me to have more children, but I don't feel I can go through with it without him. Alan I think you are trying to do too much for us." the Queen stated.

"No, a people that have produced as beautiful and loving a soul as Hopix, someone I feel that has rescued me from a private hell I was in deserves more, much more than I have done." Alan told her with as serious a face as he could. The Queen could only nod to that, Hopix was all that, and more even the Queen had to admit that Hopix was a rarity these days with all the evil that had befallen all of them. "I have to go Glimmer but we need to discuss this more." Alan said as another Fairixie motioned for Alan to follow.

Walking into the room, he saw that the lizard guy was still going through his own private hell, smiling Alan delved in standing like a solid rock in a sea of chaos. The screams were almost deafening; pointing, and raising his hand the lizard guy rose from the bottom of the chaos. "So are you ready to end this? Or do you want more? Believe me there is so much more the total amount of people that you killed on the Triboc world alone would take years to experience." When the lizard guy still did nothing, but gasp and cry, Alan looked him straight in the eyes.

"Just remember you are the one that caused all this pain I feel it is only fair that you share in what you and you only caused." When the lizard guy still said nothing Alan just shrugged and lowered his hand.

"NO! PLEASE, NO MORE! I'll talk, I'll talk." Alan listened as he started to name at least twenty five Fairixies. The one that angered him the most was

Glimix.

Between clenched teeth Alan hissed at the man, "I should leave you here while I clear these people, she is innocent! You disgust me!" With that, Alan let the man drop into the many arms that were reaching for him.

"NO! NO! YOU PROMISED!" The man started to scream.

"No I didn't, I said nothing of the sort," lifting the crying and shrieking man Alan pulled him close. "If there are any more that you haven't told me about," here Alan smiled, "this will seem like nothing I will let them ALL have you. I don't think even I can bring you out of that and there are so many; believe me if you survived I would be very surprised. Now then, are there any others?" Alan asked barely able to contain his anger.

The man nodded and then whispered the name, Alan's eyes grew wide, and then with a growl he dropped the man. "If that is all I will be back, again enjoy, you son of a bitch!" Smiling Alan started to leave as the man's screams again rose to a fever pitch.

Alan went to the first Fairixie that the man had named reaching in he found the set of orders that had been left there by the Lizard guy. Withdrawing he tried to detect the additional thoughts, it took quite a while but Alan finally got a reading. Satisfied Alan delved back in and carefully erased what shouldn't be there. Slowly he eliminated all the agent orders that the lizard guy had planted. The whole time he'd been feeling for others that might also be affected but nothing.

Sighing the last two were going to be the most difficult, though he wasn't personally connected to any of the others, it had been hard. Glimix was a different story he'd been in her mind before, having healed so much the young Fairixie deserved to be free, truly free after all the horror she'd been through.

"Glimix," he said as he approached her and her mother the Queen. Alan had already explained what he had to do to her mother as carefully as he could.

"Mazey Alan?" Glimix stated shocked when she couldn't move. Then a mask of rage came over her face, "release me you weak, pitiful, spineless Tribod" Alan could only smile, the piece of the Lizard guy was trapped, and dying as it spoke.

"That's funny I found that you are the spineless one using a helpless female to do your dirty work. Tsk, Tsk, Tsk, too bad you're already dead you just don't realize it yet." Alan waited then a moment later a scream escaped Glimix's lips as she collapsed. Alan sat her gently to the side, covering her trembling body; reaching out he could see that she was now free.

Turning to the Queen Alan smiled, "she is clear Glimmer, I thought for a moment I might lose her." Alan groaned as the Queen also found that she was frozen and was struggling to break free, Alan was surprised that she hadn't detected him in her mind. "You really thought you'd be able to hide from me? You truly are a weak idiot!"

Glimmer's face also twisted into a mask of pure hate, "You are better than I at first thought, but there are billions out ... What have you done? NO! I will not go back to the torture! There is no way you can force me from as strong a mind as hers, she is mine, and I will never relinquish her!" An evil laugh issued from the Queen's lips.

Alan only smiled as he started to push at what the lizard guy was in the Queen's mind, "Obviously you forgot, the mind you are in is an old mind. It has limitless power to the one it belongs to, isn't that right Glimmer?"

A scream issued from her lips, "NO! I put you to sleep you have no power I control everything here!"

Another voice issued from Glimmer's lips, "I don't think so, this is my mind as Alan said I have had it a very long time and know more than a few tricks. Now get OUT!" Another scream louder this time came from her lips then died. As Glimmer started falling, Alan caught her and laid her on the couch next to her daughter. Weakly Glimmer opened her eyes and motioned for Alan to bend low to her. Lightly and lovingly she kissed his cheek, then whispered in his ear. Growling Alan nodded and whispered back to the Queen who smiled then closed her eyes to sleep.

Alan looked at the three females asleep on the couches, shaking his head he walked to Hopix and gently cupped her face as he brushed a light kiss across her lips. Suddenly Hopix's eyes snapped open, "NO! There was no way that you could know that I was here!." The lizard guy screamed unable to move.

Growling between clenched teeth Alan told him, "Going after Glimix was bad enough, but then you went after the Queen also. Going after Hopix was the last straw there is no where you can go now but back into your own body. I made you a promise, I keep my promises. Kiss your ass good bye!"

Laughing evilly the Lizard guy decided to play his last card, "I'd rethink that! You obviously don't see what I have a hold of, move me, and she dies! Leave me, and she lives, maybe. Now then, you are ... what is happening? NO! No you can't I put you away where you couldn't interfere!"

"As with the Queen, I have had my mind for a while and I also know where to hide 'til Alan released me. You truly are a stupid being trying to attack us. We are well acquainted with our own minds, as the Queen said it is time for you to GET OUT!" With that the man screamed high pitched then was gone. "Thank you Alan again you have saved me. I love you so much, thank yo ... u."

Alan breathed a sigh of relief finally it was over there was only one thing left to do, well two actually. Alan stood and rubbed his eyes shit he was tired but he needed to watch over these three 'til they awoke. A few hours later Glimix and Glimmer both opened their eyes. Both were shocked that they were laying down then the memories flooded in, and they looked at Alan with looks of love and appreciation. Then, they both noticed that Hopix was also there, but she should also be awake. Alan smiled at both of them feeling so bone weary he had to be here when Hopix awoke.

"I was about to suggest that you rest, but I can see that you wouldn't listen. Hopix is truly lucky that you two have found each other." Glimmer got up to leave then noticed that Glimix hadn't moved,

"Come, Glimix leave them there will be time later."

Though she whined a bit, Glimix listened to her mother and rose to leave with her. Stopping a moment, she ran back to Alan throwing her arms around him, "Thank you Mazey Alan, you have saved me again," looking at Hopix she looked back at Alan, "Please take good care of her she is a very dear friend." With that she kissed Alan on the cheek and ran back to her mother. Alan rubbed his cheek where she'd kissed him, a look of true wonder on his face.

It wasn't long after that that Hopix awoke, stretching she looked around. "The Queen and Glimix are gone?" She asked.

Alan nodded, "For some reason, I think they wanted us to have some time together. We haven't had that much time alone for a while; I think it was an extremely nice gesture."

Hopix smiled and then thought she just hoped Alan felt that way when the full truth came out, then she felt the love that he had for her and knew it really didn't matter. She didn't think it really would to Alan either well ... at least she hoped.

Alan held Hopix close his feelings for her had jumped substantially in the past few weeks, looking down he groaned. She was still in her Fairixie clothes that really left nothing to the imagination, the fact that her breasts were half exposed wasn't helping either. Plus her skirt was so short it showed off more than just a little of her perfectly smooth legs that almost called him to caress them. Tearing his eyes away, his manhood rose to the occasion, his pants again tented as he had to turn and adjust before she noticed. He was just glad that they would be married soon but knew he had to find the Queen's husband before he and Hopix could be united as a couple.

Looking closer at her face he couldn't find a single flaw with it the skin was smooth, her voice always had him feeling as if he could do anything.

"Hopix? I have to call the council, there is a mission I feel I have to do. I feel I owe the Queen and your people so much that I have to do it." Alan told her a few moments later having to tear his gaze away from her face.

"I understand, Alan I will do all I can to help you as I always do." Hopix said with a wide smile on her face. "What mission is it?"

"I want to go after the Queen's husband," he told her as her mouth hung open, going after the Queen's husband but no one had seen or heard from him in over 3 thousand years!

"Alan there is no guarantee that he is even alive we've always been told that he was a mage not unlike you." Hopix told him.

"I know Hopix but I have felt the pain that the Queen has, a deep and empty pain that lingers and festers there in the dark growing stronger the longer it is there. I too have this pain but thanks to you and your people I am slowly defeating it. One day I hope that I can completely defeat it but for now I am far better than I was." Alan told her a wide smile on his face, yes his love for her was definitely starting to overcome the pain left by his wife.

"I think I understand Alan, still I will help you all I can. I am your partner as long as you wish."

Hopix told him.

Alan's face suddenly lit up, "I wish for you to always be my partner Hopix, with the missions or cases and in life unite with me Hopix as my mate. I feel so complete with you by my side; I never want to be separated from you again."

Hopix's mouth was hanging open Alan wanted to unite with her in a union? Suddenly Hopix's heart began to beat faster. A warm feeling spread all over her body as she started to blush. (Alan found it so adorable). "You ... I ... but ... but..." suddenly quiet but with the biggest smile he'd ever seen on her face Alan gently grasped her face again and kissed her as deeply as he could pouring all of himself into the kiss, he felt Hopix almost collapse against him then groan as the passion began to overtake her. Breaking the kiss they both were in a daze only capable of staring at each other.

As always someone was always there to muck things up, as they both heard someone clearing their throat behind them. "Really Alan you should think more on things before you open your mouth, making promises that your body may not be able to keep." Alan and Hopix both recognized the voice of the Fairixie council member.

"Nealiex!" Hopix squealed grasping the other in a fierce hug. "It has been too long since you were home my dear friend!"

Nealiex's wide smile was infectious as Alan began to smile at the scene. "Why are you here Nealiex? Is the council trying to think up new ways to further torture me?" Alan growled though only halfhearted.

"I was told that Hopix had finally given her heart and soul to someone," here the Fairixie pointed a slender finger at Alan. "You had better take great care of my friend, don't break her heart or you might have the wrath of me coming down upon you!" Laughing, she skipped away, with Hopix laughing even harder at Alan's look of concern and confusion.

"He is absolutely adorable Hopix!" He heard Nealiex tell Hopix, "No I am not here to torture you, if anything I am here to help you. As the council leader warned, I must warn you that the dark council will stop at nothing to end you and all the work you have done. You have already shifted the balance towards being even again. They have promised that they will take you down, I'd expect more rogue agents trying to get back in with the dark council."

"So you're telling me that the rules are about to change?" Sighing Alan nodded, "Yup that's about how I figured it would be, as always." Throwing his hands up in defeat, "Nothing is ever easy it seems now."

Alan watched as the two friends embraced and sat talking about everything that had happened lately.

Sitting down, Alan realized that he'd been away from earth almost constantly now for at least a week. I'm going to get lazy he thought being off planet so much with these powers. Putting his hands in his pocket, he leaned back against the wall he'd been sitting on. His eyes were almost closed when his fingers brushed over the face of the cube.

Suddenly Alan gasped out seeing a human man lying unconscious on a pallet that seemed to be sealed with a clear, Alan wasn't sure what it was. Looking close he could see that the man was alive but extremely slow. What the hell? Jerking up from the vision, Alan could also see that the man was very close to dying! He had to go now or it would be too late!

Nearby, Queen Glimmer gasp out, she'd seen what Alan had pulled up with the cube. Huge tears were streaming down her face he was alive! Though it appeared not much longer. At least she got to see him one last time. His mouth agape, Alan could feel the Queen watching him, "I have to go now, Glimmer to have a chance," Alan said to the cube. The Queen nodded as she watched Alan stand and walk to the council member and Hopix.

"I'm sorry to break this up but we have to go now Hopix! I just saw the Queen's husband and he is still alive. He won't be much longer if I can't reach him." Alan told both of them bowing low but trying to urge them to move faster. Hopix's mouth was open in surprise as she stood moving to Alan.

Nealiex also bowed to Alan, bringing a few gasps from a few passing by. "Please be careful; you are our best agent since the Queen's husband." Alan nodded, then took Hopix's hand nodding to Nealiex again then they both vanished. "I just hope that you can accomplish this, my dear friends," Nealiex said to herself as she too vanished.

Appearing again in what he could only describe as a mass of almost solid clouds; Alan shook his head and concentrated. Soon everything appeared to look like more familiar to him. They'd only taken a few steps when a vision assailed them.

"Hold Triacarie! You are not welcome here; leave while you still can!" Alan, who had his feelers out the whole time, began to laugh.

"You really expect me to be scared away by a mere student? Are you such a coward that you have to hide behind the skirts of a little female?" A roar sounded then several fireballs (sighing Alan shook his head, nothing original still) bounced off his shields. "Wow," Alan started, "that was really pathetic!" Here Alan laughed even harder almost falling on the ground at how weak the blasts had been.

"Tell you what," Alan stated to the vision, "just come here and let me destroy you so I am not wasting my time with a pitiful ... thing like you." There was another roar then the ugh! All Alan knew was that it looked like a green slimy slug with arms and legs. Oh yeah, he forgot the bulging eyes on top.

"You dare to insult me? This is the dark council's world I think you will find it extremely difficult to win here." The green creature said.

To which Alan started to laugh even harder, "Please, I destroyed 10 of you asses on the sister Fairixie world this shouldn't be that difficult."

The creature smiled, (Alan thought it was a smile was too hard to tell). "Ah! You are the one that destroyed them, you might find it much more of a challenge here we know what to expect!" Here the creature began to laugh again.

"I see you really don't know who you are dealing with," Alan told the creature right before he reached out and started to rip and shred everything he felt that was magic in it. Screaming the being tried to flash out and then lash out, suddenly finding it had no power.

"NO! Stay away from me! I'd rather give myself to the council than submit to you!" The creature yelled at Alan, shaking his head. Alan backed off as the dark council arrived and started to rip all the life from the creature. Alan turned and started to walk away.

"Alan Glanto," he heard and turned eyeing the dark council, "you have freed a small very small section of this world. Realize this we have held this world a very long time; there are well over one hundred mages here, all loyal to us, all ready to kill for us. " here the leader indicated what was left of the slug being, "was one of the weakest." Drawing closer to Alan, almost in Alan's face the dark leader continued. "They are ready for you here, one hundred well ninety nine mages, plus they all have at least one apprentice. You are strong, yes though I doubt you are that strong."

Alan returned the favor getting in the leader's face and replying, "I am a hell of a lot more than you think I am. I also know of your plan for the battle on earth. Remember you have lost twenty four of your best agents that can travel to earth. If you remember I took 20 of them out at one time you really want to see how many you can lose if I actually get upset?!" The look of shock, then hatred on the leader's face made Alan smile. "Good I'm glad we understand each other."

Turning again Alan thought a moment then turned back, "Don't think I have forgotten the rules either. I know I am alone, but we'll see, won't we?"

This last dig really pissed off the leader and several of the council members as they growled and the dark council vanished.

Alan looked back at Hopix, "I really wish the cube would take me to the spot where he is." Shaking his head Alan stated, "I swear I never get a break though destroying one at the start helps." Here Alan smiled at Hopix who was staying close to Alan a look of fear on her face as she looked everywhere.

Alan noticed this and pulled her close, suddenly she calmed and to Alan's shock he could feel her power almost double! Hell yeah! Alan thought she had major ass kicking potential now. Reaching out Alan started to stretch his feelings outward looking for the man he'd come here for. That's when he felt a small group of ... well he wasn't sure what they were moving toward them. Ah! Crap Alan thought I forgot about them!

It seemed like a small army of beings that reminded him a lot of the Tribocs same yellow skin, same three mouths, though these only had three eyes and were a good foot taller. All of them saw Alan, walked to him, and bowed, sighing he'd been afraid of this.

"Rise, I am not here to rule you, only to free you." Passing a hand over all of them, Alan had cleared almost all of them when he felt two in the back whose minds refused to be free. Sighing Alan saw that they were just like those on the sister Fairixie world who could not except that they were free. Saddened, Alan waved his hand and sent them to another area where they could be brought to the leader of that area.

Clearing the ... whatever it was where the bad mage had lived. Alan made a new home for the free ... what in the hell was he to call them? Calling the obvious leader to the front Alan explained what he was doing, he also asked what they were called.

"Triacarie, when I was a youngling, when the dark ones started to come here, I remember we called ourselves Lobrits. It has been a very long time since we were called that. We realize that you are different; no other has ever helped us to be free. As for the one you seek, we have heard of a still free clan many deres over that way." The leader and several of the older Lobrits bowed low to Alan and walked into the now small village that Alan had created. Shaking his head he'd only taken a few steps after they were all in when another slimey slug looking creature appeared in front of him.

"Ha! You are so dead, you bastard, kill one of us and we all will not stop 'til you are dead!" It spit at him, Alan smirked he wasn't stupid he knew a set up when he saw it. Felling around, hmmm six of them huh?

"You know," Alan told the creature in front of him, "you guys are pathetic!" With that Alan fired at all six that he felt around him. All six were dead within moments shaking his head he took another step then fired off another three shot. Christ! Didn't these guys even know how to hide their power?

"Alan," Hopix whispered to him, "I think all but one of them were apprentices."

"So they are trying to find out how strong I really am," looking around, sure he was being watched Alan shouted. "As I stated before you guys are really pathetic, I'm not even at one-fourth power you are making it easier for me later. Oh well it's your death!"

Alan started to walk again not really expecting any more attacks, he'd only gone a few feet when he felt another ten appear nearby. Hmmm he thought these are most definitely not weak like the others. Upping his shield Alan kept going 'til the first fired at him, then the second, then the rest all (really? fireballs you'd think they'd learned by now he was VERY strong against them, wouldn't you?) Sighing Alan targeted the first 3 and then they were gone. The other seven kept going thinking that Alan was weakening.

"I suggest that unless you want to die, you one, stop and two, go away!" When neither happened Alan shook his head well, he'd warned them. Reaching out all seven screamed as they were destroyed at the same time. Looking at Hopix Alan shrugged, "I warned them they had a chance."

Hopix looked at Alan with new respect she'd felt no strain or stress when they were firing at Alan on his shield. Her eyes wide she knew that Alan wouldn't let anything happen to her, but she hadn't thought he was THIS powerful! Hugging him she said, "Yes you did Alan I guess they thought they could beat you, their mistake. That leaves at least 88, can you clear all of their slaves?"

Reaching out Alan could see that these guys had less than the last guy; all 10 put together had almost the same as the one guy. Crap, this will take a while if he had to release them all. Waving his arm they were all suddenly there, pointing to the village he expanded it into a small town. Again Alan was releasing all of the new Lobrits when he again came across 20 that refused to be freed, sending them elsewhere Alan related what he was doing and that the now larger town was for them. Watching them go Alan strengthened the protection over the town, just hope it holds he thought.

They were maybe a half mile from the town when another group of the Lobrits met them. These seemed different as they had no blank stares and they were all armed. Stopping short Alan waited to see what they would do, for a few minutes they stared at each other. Then Alan guessed that it was the leader who slowly approached him.

"Are you a Triacarie?" The strange creature asked him.

"I do not know what that word means; I can understand you but that word holds no meaning for me." Alan told the now stunned leader.

"We were charged to come here at this time to retrieve a Triacarie, though the word that was written was ma ... ge." Alan's eyes opened wide; this was the first time he'd been called that off earth.

"Where did you see this? It is a word that is used on my world. It means one who possesses magic abilities dealing with power from the elements and planet." Alan told the even more shocked Leader.

Bowing low the leader said, "It is as was foretold; please come with us the first one is close to death. Nothing our healers do can bring him closer to life. It was foretold that another of his race would come one day and release him and our world though many would die before it was over. Already we have felt the lessening of the darkness on our world."

Alan and Hopix both looked at each other it was foretold? What in the hell was going on? They walked for a short distance then the ground opened and they all went down into a narrow passage way. It only took a minute or so then they were in a huge cavern type of room.

"Where are we?" Alan asked as soon as they stopped.

"We are in..." The leader stopped when another of the Lobrits walked up to him and excitedly started talking to him. As they went on, the leader's eyes grew wider then he dismissed the other and turned to Alan. "I have been informed that you have destroyed a whole sector of the evil Triacarie and freed all the slaves they had. You also provided a safe place for all of them." The leader fell at Alan's feet crying, "My family is in part of the sector, I was informed that all but one of them are in the place."

Alan tried to lift the being off the floor feeling that he'd not really done anything. Still the being was crying as were several in the room, all bowing on the floor to Alan. "Please stop!" Alan said a little more forceful than he intended. "I only did what was right, I am not a god I am just a plain being like you."

All of the Lobrits looked up at Alan like he was crazy; he'd done what hadn't been done in a very long time. "I need to see the first one as you called him before he is no longer."

The leader got to his feet and quickly ushered Alan and Hopix to where the man was.

Looking down on him, Alan had a strange feeling he knew the man but couldn't place him for his life. Reaching out Alan tried to heal the man but it seemed that the clear covering over the man was preventing anything from reaching him magic included.

Looking at Hopix Alan started, "I need you to lift the clear shell then I can start in on his healing. Tell me if you can't hold it long ok?" Alan said smiling to her.

"I am a lot stronger now than I was Alan," she smirked at him.

Alan nodded to Hopix as she lifted the clear cover, the man inside began to gasp, and Alan threw all he had into healing all the failing organs, a few minutes later the man was finally breathing better. Taking the clear enclosure from her Alan sat a moment to rest the man was no longer on death's door but he wasn't all that well yet either. Alan shook his head almost all of the man's organs had been about to fail, both of his lungs were on the verge of collapse. Almost all of the bones in the body were broken; the only area that was unaffected was the brain.

Alan had all the bones from the neck to the waist healed, at least now if the man awoke there wouldn't be as much pain. This was the most extreme healing he'd ever done good thing he'd healed a lot before of this would be almost impossible. Alan had finally finished one leg and was half done with the other when the man's eyes slowly opened.

Shocked momentarily, the man nodded at Alan then Hopix, "Glad you're finally here Alan."

Alan's mouth hung open who in the hell was this guy? "Excuse me," Alan started, "do we know each other?"

"No I'm afraid that we've never met before." The man smiled, "Glad you are as good at healing as you are."

"Uh huh," Alan said as he looked at the man damn but he reminded him of someone he'd seen before.

"Oh I'm sorry Alan, I forgot to introduce myself Myrddin, Myrddin Wyllt. Ah I see you don't know that hmmm ok, just call me Merlin then." Alan almost missed the man when his mouth dropped open WHAT!!????

PART 3

CHAPTER 1

Alan did his best to steady his hands, Merlin!? THE MERLIN? What in the hell was going on? Was there truth in almost all of the old legends? Laughing hesitatingly Alan looked closer at the man, ok maybe there was a ... little resemblance to the man of legend.

"Wait, wait, wait," Alan started out, "you're The Merlin? King Arthur? Camelot and the round table? All of that?"

"Well yes, is there another magic user on earth called Merlin?" The man smirked, though it was hard to tell with the long growth of his beard the man had.

Alan stopped and turned toward Hopix, "I thought you said that the earth now has a dampening effect on all magic users? That was the reason I couldn't..."

"A dampening effect? Only on Magic users?" The man was saying as he tried to sit up still stiff from not having moved in over a thousand years. "Sounds suspiciously like what happened in my time. That bitch Morgan le Fay was learning magic at an alarming rate. I found out later that promises of the dark council seduced her."

Alan had stopped for a moment causing Merlin to turn and see the look of pain and great distrust on Alan's face.

"Ah, I see that you are well acquainted with them! A real nasty lot for sure." Merlin stared at Alan harder a moment longer then nodded, "So you know how properly to deal with them, I see, and the fact that you caught them in a lie, and used that against them was genius my boy. Though I would caution you not to do it too often they always seem to find a way to turn the tables on you I know for a fact as you can see. Oh yes, this was their work."

The whole time Alan was taking in every word the man was saying he had been at this far longer than he had and with less power to boot! "I've been told you came here a very long time ago," Alan told the man. "As outnumbered as you are, you think the white council would have helped."

Here the man lowered his head, "I'm afraid that they didn't know at the time 'til it was almost too late. By the time they placed me in the chamber, the planet was already in the hands of the dark council. I am afraid it was all they could do, had they taken me they would have been in violation of their own rules they set down."

Alan could only smile he was really starting to like this man! He'd kept the council in the dark. Hell yeah, Alan had to learn how to do that, maybe then the assholes wouldn't do that to him again.

Merlin could only smile he could almost see the thoughts that the younger man had going through his head. It might be good to teach the man some of his tricks, might make his job easier and a lot more fun that's for sure!

"So my good man though almost all the pain is gone I still can't walk, bum leg and all." Merlin informed Alan. Alan nodded and started back healing the leg; the man was almost whole again within minutes. Standing the man patted Alan on the back, "Thank you my good man now," Merlin slapped his hands together rubbing them together. "It's time to get back to work!"

Alan passed a hand over Merlin effectively freezing the man. "I think not Merlin; I just brought you back from near death. I'm not about to let you try and temp fate again ok? Stay here for a bit I'll go kill a few then we'll talk ok?"

"You're a damn sure fire, cocky bastard aren't you?" Merlin spat at Alan.

Alan stopped a moment then turned to Merlin with a huge smile on his face, "Yes, you might say that, I have to be or I'd most definitely be dead right now. Just stay here and rest you haven't been out there in a very long time the little I have done today has barely affected the balance on this world." Alan walked up to Merlin and with a deadly serious look told the older man, "I damn sure intend to change that!"

Merlin watched as Alan walked away, a wide smile crossing his face, so it was true! The one had finally been born and arrived. Sighing Merlin sat down if the man actually could kill a few more then they had a chance. With the removal of the weakest twelve plus their apprentices, Alan might not feel a difference but he most definitely could.

Alan and Hopix exited the underground cavern; Alan stood there a moment wondering who he should go after.

"Hey asshole!" Alan heard from behind him, (again?!) A fireball bounced off his shield.

Well, that solved that problem, "Ok, here's the deal, you can leave or stay and die! Your choice." Alan could feel another what? Twenty? Thirty? They too felt as pathetic as those before. Must have sent their apprentices again. Shaking his head Alan just extended his arm then lifted it, might as well see who he was killing. As the thirty bodies flailed about in the air Alan again repeat his earlier warning. "Same deal, stay and die. Well?"

All of the thirty began to spit, and curse at him in several languages, nodding with a sigh Alan closed his hand and all thirty popped out of existence. The one that had fired at Alan started to blubber and scurry away. Alan made a slashing motion and the last dropped dead. "Damn it! The pansies are sending their apprentices out after me. They obviously think I am like Merlin and am weakening. I put the remaining eighty seven of you on notice I am coming for you! Don't..." Alan started when several bolts of electricity hit his shield, about time! Alan thought.

"You wanted us asshole we're here; think you can take all of us? We aren't the weak pathetic creatures you have faced before," came a voice behind a hill.

"So, are we going to see each other? Or are you going to hide? I actually like to see who the hell I kill when I eradicate pure evil!" Alan said as he made a flattening motion and the hill was as flat as the land around it. Behind it were several slimy orange blobs and a few creatures that reminded Alan of piranha walking on two legs.

"Ha you are so dead! We are nothing compared to our parents!" One of the orange blobs spit at Alan.

"Good! I am tired of dealing with weak examples of those that are in power here!" With that Alan waved a hand and the ten in front of him simply screamed then vanished into a dust. Damn! Alan thought even when they are dead they are dirtying up the place! Alan heard a gasp then he felt Hopix's power skyrocket suddenly there was a scream then Hopix was rushing to his side.

"I ... I ... killed one Alan oh god! I think I am going to be sick!" Hopix said when she reached him. Really? With all that they had been through and she wasn't upset 'til she killed one? Shaking his head Alan looked out at all the places he could feel the others hiding.

"Ok, same deal as before as always. You leave you live, stay here and get slaughtered. There are only nineteen of you left. I took out ten of you easily you nineteen really think you are strong enough to defeat me? As I said leave and live stay and well ... you'll be dead soon so guess it doesn't matter. I'll give you a minute that's all." Alan didn't really expect them to give up but he was always fair he had to give them a chance.

A few moments later all nineteen advanced on Alan firing a variety of different bolts, waves, and yes (sigh) fireballs. Alan could only smirk when he didn't even feel them hitting his shield; he gave them a chance.

Slashing at his throat eight fell bleeding from their throats, undaunted the others renewed their attacks. Sighing at how stupid they were Alan crushed another five watching the others walk over the screaming corpses. The last six were definitely in a higher class of mage; smiling Alan threw several knife shaped bolts at all five. After four of the remaining six went down Alan nodded, so these weren't just weak ones any more, good!

"I see we are found out, no matter," one of the last two said. "Now feel true power!" With that a huge bolt of ice and frigid cold struck his shield. On the other side a huge wave of water fell on his shield freezing solid in a mere second. Alan nodded not bad he was near one half power, barely enough for his power to grow a little. Smiling though they didn't need to know that.

Outside the water user was laughing," he'll never escape that! No one freezes as deeply as you! He'll be dead long..." there was a slight cracking sound then the ice exploded outwards sending thousands of razor sharp shards away from Alan.

The water user screamed and tried to flash out but was caught by one thousand or more of the shards as they shredded part of his chest, and the rest of the right side of his body. The ice wielder just smiled as he absorbed the ice that flew at him. So this was no wimp they had sent an actual mage not a fake like the last one he'd nearly killed. Good it would be actually be a challenge! Flashing out before Alan had a clear line of sight on him, Alan cursed when he saw that the last one had gotten away.

Hopix curled up next to Alan tears falling from her eyes. Looking at her he held her close and waited, he knew they should be alone before long they always were. It seemed that as a byproduct of defeating them the slaves that they had held on to were brought to where he was. Sure enough a few minutes later a rather large mass of dazed and confused group of the Lobrits appeared.

Alan waved both of his arms creating a small city that had once stood here, and then came the process of clearing them though as he'd thought before it was getting easier to do larger and larger groups. Alan could see that there were about five thousand almost twice what he'd done last time, reaching out he did the first thousand with no problem the same with the second and third thousand, He was half way through the last two thousand when he began to find those that refused the freedom he offered. He was already at one hundred fifty and the number was starting to climb.

"Damn it! Hopix this is going to take longer than I want to. I'm already over two hundred who want to remain a slave to these assholes!" Alan told Hopix with an exasperated sigh.

Once he hit five hundred, he shook his head and sent a shock wave through those left. Well, over half of those left fell Jerking and shrieking. Alan cleared the rest and sent them to the rest of those in the city. Alan counted nine hundred eighty eight who had refused to let go and accept freedom.

Alan was suddenly tired of fighting these assholes, tired of no life, hell he was just tired of being tired! Looking around, Alan started sending those on the ground to other areas.

Looking at Hopix Alan nodded that he was done. Hopix could see the bone weariness in his eyes; they had been at this for over a month now, almost non - stop. Even she had to admit she was starting to grow weary with the constant fighting, hiding, and freeing of different worlds. When it was her world she had been tireless now, she was just weary.

Alan flashed them back to the underground sanctuary, even the warriors who had come to welcome them stood back. They knew some of what Alan and Hopix had been through, though they sympathized there was far too much at stake for them to rest. Much as when Hopix had been trying to free her world, they didn't have time to be tired or exhausted.

Alan walked into where Merlin was resting taking a cot on the other side of the room. Laying down a heavy sigh escaped his lips. Though not as powerful as Alan, Merlin could recognize and feel that Alan was exhausted more than he wanted to admit. Especially after today, Merlin had felt Alan come up against the last one he'd fought.

Reaching out, Merlin could now truly feel the balance of the planet starting to shift. Though he'd taken out forty-one nearly half of those here, he'd only gotten five of the middle strength mages. The fifty-nine that were left wouldn't be a walk in the woods that was for sure. Smiling Merlin could see quite a lot from the powerful young mage including the love he had for a certain young Fairixie, yes this was very interesting!

Merlin walked out through the back door he'd made well over a thousand years ago. True he wasn't as strong but he had a brain and more than a few tricks that he could use to get some of them. Damn that young mage anyway, this had been his mission and by the great power of the universe he was going to see it through. Besides he'd already picked up a little of the ability that the young mage Alan had. He could already feel his power slowly increasing, not a lot, but possibly enough to keep him alive until Alan felt better. Kneeling outside Merlin prayed to an ancient named power that he'd make it and one day get to see his wondrous Glimmer again.

Making his way Merlin set a low shield around his self, Ah! Good it was as he thought even low power helps increase the young mage's nice ability. No wonder he was so tired to get where he is now he'd have to have been going for well over a month straight! Hell even he'd be exhausted after a month of that much intensity!

Merlin approached the middle level mage's home, I just hope I don't muck this up Merlin thought any I take out should help the young mage.

Merlin had lowered all his power but had them set to snap up at a moment's notice, hmmm even pushing his power down was causing them to slightly increase. My, Merlin thought, I keep this up and should be a middle-level mage in no time! Knocking at the ... Merlin guessed it was a door he felt a weak power approaching.

The ... door opened an ant shaped creature gasped then died in a ball of flame. There was a rasping sound as Merlin hid then another bigger ant looking creature appeared beside the ashes.

"This was no accident, but I feel no one here, strange the idiot must have been practicing his... " Merlin hit the creature with everything he had. Screaming, the creature tried too late to erect a shield, then withered as the flames quickly ate the creature up. Smiling

Merlin thought well, that helps, but I better go! A moment later Merlin was one thousand yards away. What! He'd never been able to muster more than one hundred feet! What had he gotten from the young mage? Though tired, Merlin thought of getting away again and was another one thousand yards further!

Merlin walked back in the back door and lay down, god he was tired; that had taken so much out of him, but he could feel several of his abilities now at middle level. Finally, he could do more than just trick the bastards! Merlin closed his eyes he had to rest he still wasn't used to the amount of power his body had produced.

An hour later Alan awoke, god that had helped so much! Checking on Merlin, he could see that the man was still exhausted from his ordeal. Alan had been hoping to take him out today so the man could show him some of the tricks that had kept him alive. Shrugging Alan walked out to find that many of the Lobrits there were excited, it seemed that last night one of the evil Triacaries had been killed without raising an alarm, and there had been no sign of a battle or struggle. The other Triacaries were as baffled as the Lobrits were.

Many looked at Alan but knew that he'd been

resting last night, worn out from all he'd done the day before. Hopix came to Alan a moment later, "I went there with the patrol when we heard, I at first thought it had been you also but I didn't feel you there. It was a mage that much I am sure of but one I am not familiar with. You think you could find out?" Hopix asked Alan.

Ok what in the hell was going on? Thing is he'd had that strange ass dream last night like it had been him but not him. Sighing Alan nodded as he and Hopix headed to where the mage had lived. The closer they got the more certain Alan was that he'd been here before but that was impossible! He hadn't moved all night and as far as he knew his energy self had stayed also so who in the hell had done this?

Looking over everything Alan could still see the attack from last night, everything 'til whoever it was had flashed out. Hmmmm Alan had an idea but he wasn't that sure, he'd have to check tonight then he'd know for sure.

They'd just finished and were starting back when several of the evil mages from the planet appeared. One more powerful than the rest stepped forward, "This was a good trick, don't think it will be that easy next time that is if you survive!" The spokesman backed off as the others, and then he started to fire at Alan. At half power Alan smiled so then, they were out of weak ones! Just past half power Alan just stood there, hardly feeling their blasts.

Finally, they stopped to regroup, "Ok guys, same deal leave and I won't mess with you as long as you leave me alone. Stay and I'll just have to destroy you. Your choice."

"Leave? And do what? I worked all my life only to be spit on by the same people that wanted me to be a Clintarie. I killed all of them their screams are the only thing that brought me peace. In the words of your world shove your deal up your ass!" The spokesman said with most of the other 10 nodding in agreement.

"Fine then," As Alan reached in and crushed all the magic the leader had. "That was easy; from what I felt, he was the strongest. Now then same deal. What's your decision?" There were a few moments that only the screams of the leader could be heard then the nine remaining started to fire at Alan again. Alan sadly shook his head, killing four of them with a blast of energy. The remaining five tried to run and would have made it, but Alan caught four, effectively crushing them. The last flashed out Alan just shook his head, he might as well prepare for the Lobrits that he knew would be coming soon.

Alan had already cleared an area and had just finished erecting another small city when there was a sudden rush of power. The same man from the day before appeared, holding the one that had gotten away by the throat. "Hello Alan, I just thought you'd like to see that he really didn't get away, oh by the way that was a good trick last night. Seriously though don't think it will work on the rest of us. Ah! Here they come. Masters." The man thing bowed to the dark council.

"Very good Tnavres, Nam Daed you knew the penalty for what you did yet you thought to hide from us! Your soul is ours Dead Man!" The leader of the dark Council shrieked as all twelve of them descended upon the man screaming and shrieking himself. Among the evil laughs Alan could hear the ripping and tearing of the man's flesh and soul as both were devoured. "Ah, it's always good to have an early soul, but nowhere as good as yours when we take it, Alan Glanto!"

"Well, you can try but as you see you are losing, that one made fifty-nine, I know, I Know they weren't the most powerful. Then again they were nothing and they were the middle of the middle level. Just like your pathetic!" Alan said trying to bait the leader of the council hell the entire council for that matter!

The leader and several of the council smiled wicked evil smiles, "There won't be a way out this time Alan Glanto at least not for you! Beware as you said these were pathetic, but they were nothing compared to our Champion!"

The creature that had appeared with the escaping man threw a blast at Alan. Smiling Alan brought up almost all his shields at full. At first Alan just looked at the creature as he started to increase his power. Ten minutes later Alan saw that the creature was struggling as was he. Firing off a full blast, the creature could barely deflect though it still singed his arm a bit.

Finally stopping the creature turned to the dark council, "finally! A combatant worthy of my power as I feel I am of his! Wonderful! I sir, will thoroughly enjoy killing your ass!" With a flourish, the creature vanished.

"So no bets. I see you must be afraid that I will kill your Champion leaving you with nothing; not unlike you have now!" Alan said pressing the matter; they might know what he is doing but that didn't mean he still couldn't get them to lose it and say something stupid again.

"Nice try but we know we will win, no sense betting what we know will be ours soon. Goodbye Alan Glanto it wasn't a pleasure meeting you, but it will be eating your soul." The leader said a wide smile on his face.

Alan started to laugh, looked at the council, and laughed harder. "What have you found to be so funny?" The leader asked.

"You and how ridiculous you sound. After I defeat all of these assholes I imagine that I won't be able to get rid of you interfering in my life. You idiots can be such a nuisance." Alan said laughing even harder.

The leader's face contorted into a mask of rage, "Fine you little shit, you win we won't interfere in YOUR life again."

"Hell with that in any of the life of earth, or are you afraid, cause I think you are!" With that Alan turned and started to walk away.

"Fine you shit, it's settled, if you win but if we win we get both of you!" The leader spit out in a fit of rage.

Alan looked at Hopix who smiled and nodded, "Agreed, oh by the way the previous agreement stands you interfere and the deal is off and I will call for another judgment."

Grumbling the leader and several of the council nodded, then vanished to a smiling Alan. Myrddin Wyllt shook his head; the young mage was good damn good! Then there was the champion of the dark council that he had faced (and lost to most miserably) by all that is holy! Those two had gone at each other with an amount of power he could only imagine. True his own power had jumped quite a bit, he was no longer in the upper low level range, he'd passed that the first day now he'd say he was at the low end of the mid-range.

Waving his hand, Merlin flashed out and appeared near the opening at the back of the sanctuary. Smiling he could feel his power climbing a bit more, good at least now he wasn't as powerless as he was, though the champion would make short work of him. Laughing, Merlin thought Ha! At least now the bastard would actually have to work a bit to beat him (ah hell who was he fooling?) Nodding his head he continued to do all the spells he could to get his power to increase.

Alan turned when he felt the power flash out but saw nothing, so there were still a few lower power mages out there. Funny thing was though this one almost felt like Merlin but that wasn't possible as he remembered Merlin's power was very low especially compared to his. Alan could feel the throbbing in his chest as his power was increasing a bit more. Smirking, Alan thought the idiot had helped to defeat himself, Alan was already where the champion was, but now he felt he was slightly higher. Sighing Alan thought well we'll see, especially after I get rid of the higher level mages that were left.

Hopix could see that Alan was deep in thought but she had to know. "Alan I thought that after we defeated over half of the dark mages, the light council could come in here."

Alan sighed she above everyone else should know, "Usually that would be the case, but here more than half were the weak mages. The 41 left are all of a higher power and hold most of the Lobrits here as slaves. Much like on your world, but there are far more here I am afraid that they're are also strong enough to actually challenge me."

Hopix nodded then her eyes flew wide they were that strong! Throwing her arms around Alan she held him tight as she started to tremble. Odd but she suddenly had a feeling of impending doom. Alan held her tight and gently kissed her causing her to immediately calm. "We need to go to the next the sooner we free this world the sooner we can return, having fulfilled the promise I made to the queen," Alan told her as they started to walk beyond where they had fought the others last time.

Alan had elevated and was floating forward at a rapid pace; he felt the attack long before they even started. The creature appeared to be a huge six legged animal sharp teeth and shaggy nasty smelling fur covering it. "Hold! You are on my territory; therefore, you are dead, and your soul is mine!"

A bolt of electricity shot out at Alan ('bout time they tried something different!), bouncing harmlessly off Alan's shield. Smiling Alan was about to give the creature a choice when he felt several fireballs (not again!) hit his shield. Ah! He saw now another ambush.

"Ok, you three; I give you a choice to leave..." Alan started.

"Die you ass!" The two behind him screamed and began rapid firing at him. Pissed off

Alan waved a hand then made a chopping motion. One of the creatures screamed then the head left the body, the other was also screaming though he was missing at least four of its six legs. Alan watched as it tried to crawl away then lay still as it's life blood pumped out in a huge puddle under it.

"Now as I was saying before I was rudely interrupted..." Alan started again.

"I am not interested in any pathetic deal you have to offer!" The first creature sneered at Alan, "those were my sons therefore, and there will be no deal!" With that, the leader lashed out with ever-increasing power though he was barely past half power to Alan. Then the leader started to go even higher Alan finally tired of it, shot an electric bolt at the leader. After the screams stopped, Alan just walked away the charred remains still smoldering.

Turning he took Hopix's hand as they floated a few more minutes. Alan could feel the next dark mage but seemed to be struggling to locate it. Rounding a corner they found a huge cave with a huge quantity of bones outside the entrance. "This reminds me of tales I heard of on earth during Merlin's time. Huge giants I believe with one eye called a cyclops I also believe they liked to eat beings." Hopix looked at Alan like he was crazy at least 'til the twelve foot tall monster he'd described walked out of the cave.

Taking a huge sniff the Cyclops looked around, "I smell a mage! YOU! I will enjoy eating your flesh adding your power to my own. I might even be able to beat the council's champion! Tell you what you stay right there I'll crush you, make it quick then enjoy your flesh."

Alan shot a huge fireball at the giant, which just bounced off it. Laughing the giant stared at Alan, "What an idiot you are I am impervious to all magic, better get clever or you'll bore me, then I'll make your death slow and extremely painful!" Alan smiled so impervious huh?

Waving his hand a large boulder rolled past the cave into the leg of the giant. With a growl, the giant caught the boulder and was about to throw it at Alan when Alan caught him with another in the back of his legs. As he fell back the boulder he'd been holding came crashing down on his chest, effectively trapping him. "Let me up from here you maggot! I'll crush you I'll grind you slow piece by piece."

"Normally I offer a deal, but with you," Alan spit next to the giant's head, "Fuck you!" Alan waved both arms as the weight of the huge boulder began to get heavier and heavier. Walking away Alan gritted his teeth only a minute later the giant started to scream, threaten beg then there was the sickening crack as the boulder caved in the giant's chest.

Looking at the cave Alan made a few motions and buildings began to appear along with a huge wall. As he expected over eight thousand Lobrits appeared not long after he finished the city. Sighing he would have to do a massive clearing he just hoped he had the power for it. All the Lobrits stopped before Alan, looking dazed and confused as they always did.

Alan made well over a dozen motions with his hands and arms then spread his arms wide trying to encompass all those present. He quickly had well over four hundred then started to hit the snags, then it increased 'til every three out of four didn't want to go. Pissed off again Alan made more motions then shot an energy wave out effectively knocking fifteen hundred of the last two thousand out clearing those still awake he concentrated and sent the others to one of the thirty seven dark mages that were left.

Afterward, having explained and adding warnings Alan sent them into the new city, turning toward Hopix he smiled. [Uh Hopix I think I did a little too much. I'm going to try and get us back but you might need to use the cube] Hopix looked at Alan with concern as he put a hand to his head and the other holding her hand. Then they were gone they appeared a good fifty feet from the door to the sanctuary.

Alan smiled and then collapsed beside Hopix; Concentrating Hopix managed to carry him with what little power she had (she still couldn't use her full power yet). The Lobrits came out in force carrying Alan inside and to his bed. Hopix sat next to his bed feeling tired herself she knew they were almost done. She just hoped that the last secret didn't tear them apart. Laying her head on the bed she was soon asleep herself.

Merlin had seen them come in he'd been practicing he had his power right on the edge of middle mid-range. He'd found that he could now lift things a feat he'd never been able to do except for very small things. Now he was up to at least fifty to sixty pounds, plus he could move at least a mile now, which made getting back and away very useful! Looking at the two asleep he smiled he'd heard about Alan's work today after he'd left he was still amazed that the dark council hadn't detected him or had they not really considered him a threat? A smile crossed his face that was about to change!

Merlin left via the hidden back door and started to float away, it did take energy but it got you there far faster besides, he needed all he had to pull this off. An hour later he arrived at the home of his target, pulling several crystals he'd summoned, he placed them in a certain pattern knocking on the door he stepped out of sight. The moment the servant opened the door Merlin froze him then levitated him out of the way. He'd done this twice when the master of the place came out the door.

Chanting Merlin watched as the crystals started to glow then the creature couldn't move. Merlin stepped into view as the creature smiled that was 'til he found he couldn't move to protect his self. Merlin smiled as he started it on fire. Moving again out of view Merlin waited 'til he saw others coming in. Thinking of the sanctuary he found himself two miles away from the home he'd just left, shocked. Merlin tried again and found he'd moved not two but two and a half miles! He was at three and a half miles when he appeared at the back door of the sanctuary.

Merlin looked at his hands that were glowing for the first time, and then he could feel throbbing in his chest measuring his power he found he was now at the high end of the middle of the middle range.

Finally he thought I actually have enough power to do something. Walking in he saw that Alan was still asleep from clearing all the people he'd done what now, damn near ten thousand? A drop in the ocean compared to the total population, problem was could Alan handle it? Merlin knew he was nowhere near Alan's level, but soon, if he continued, he might be able to help!

CHAPTER 2

Alan and Hopix were both dreaming Alan and Hopix had just gotten married in his dream, it was their wedding night. Alan had prepared all that day and then went to penetrate her, finding only that he couldn't get through her Hymen. His mouth wide open he tried several times, then he looked at Hopix and her face changed as a wicked smile twisted her features.

"I see you are as useless as you always have been," he heard his ex wife's voice coming out of Hopix's mouth. Yelling he tried to scramble away in horror but found that Hopix was now his ex wife, equipped with claws that held him fast. Then to his horror a huge mouth appeared as he was dragged toward it, "Finally, you'll be of good use when I devour your flesh!" Pulled into the mouth Alan began to fight to no avail, as the mouth closed he could hear his ex wife's evil laugh as the mouth began to crush his body.

Hopix's dream was no better she and Alan were finally married her father had returned to watch the proceedings, the queen presiding over everything. Hopix was extremely happy and was walking toward Alan the feeling building higher and higher. Upon reaching Alan they were almost done when Alan suddenly got an odd look on his face and pushed his way past her. With an evil sneer he turned before he left the building.

"What in the hell was I thinking? Marry your repulsive ass? NEVER! To be saddled with a putrid thing like you? I THINK NOT NEVER again!" With that, he was gone his evil laugh echoing throughout the hall. Her father and the queen still smiling just shrugged. Screaming she tried to chase after Alan only to find that the champion of the dark council was holding her back and leering at her.

"No, no, no, little one it's ok, I'll use you over and over, we'll have a huge amount of children, and I'll make sure you are pregnant all the time!" The evil champion began to laugh as Hopix's clothes fell away from her wickedly. The evil being sucked in its breath reaching for her. Suddenly she was falling fighting the currents she took flight but found she was losing the fight. Then just as suddenly her eyes snapped open as she fell from where she leaning on the bed, looking at Alan she could see that he was fighting something in his sleep.

Reaching up she very gently shook Alan whispering in his ear she was there to help him just to reach out to her. In the dream Alan could hear Hopix and extended his hands toward her voice. Snapping his eyes open Alan growled, "I feel you don't worry you'll be dead soon enough!" Alan shouted to the empty air.

From nowhere, a voice responded, "I have to admit you have an extremely powerful mind, it took quite a bit of power to penetrate your defenses but now I know your weakness!" Laughing evilly the voice continued, "It will be such a pleasure to use your little whore of a mate, and use you I will!"

Smirking Alan started to laugh almost so hard that he was about to fall off the cot he was on. "Here, you considered me an idiot!" Alan said as he started to laugh even harder. "Thank you this really ought to give me motivation to kick your ass!"

"I think you are full of shit!" The voice angrily replied, "I know she is your weak point!"

"Wrong you ass! Had you really penetrated my defenses you would have seen that she IS the reason that my powers started to increase. Everything started AFTER I left her sorry ass; actually, you remind me a lot of her. Are you sure you aren't a woman?" Alan told the voice laughing even harder now at the joke he'd made at the other's expense.

Growling the voice started to shout at Alan, "You will pay for that slur you low class dog!" Alan just smiled, so the little ass was a proud male. A good thing to remember when they actually faced each other for real.

"Whatever!" Alan told the voice, then waved his hand and felt the defenses thicken 'til he no longer felt the other.

Several of the Lobrits came scrambling into the room, "Great Triacarie! Is everything alright? We heard voices and armed ourselves to aid you!" The leader said as he and several others burst into the room, each with a fierce look prepared to battle.

"All is fine now; I have strengthened the defenses around this sanctuary. You should be fine now that one is the only one I feel that could actually project in here, that won't happen anymore." Alan told all those present, causing a huge sigh of relief to escape most of their lips.

"It is no wonder you are so tired we have heard of your night raid on another of the bad Triacaries last night. We feel so fortunate that you have come to help us, again we thank you as well for saving as many of our families as you have." Almost all of the Lobrits in the room bowed low to the floor in front of Alan.

"Please, as I said I am just a simple being like the rest of you. I am no god to be praised or worshiped." Alan told the multitude that had started to amass at the entrance to the room. Many were staring at Alan as if he'd lost his mind of course he was a god! He more than deserved to be praised, but if he wanted to be treated like any other being then so be it the really didn't want to risk his wrath.

So, Alan thought there had been another that had been killed last night, hmmm, things were starting to get interesting, there was only one other white mage here and he was a very low power mage. Or was he? Alan really began to wonder after all Merlin had come here all those centuries ago to try and do what Alan was trying to do. Then again, to do what was described, the attacker would have had to be at least a high end middle range mage or he'd had no chance to succeed.

Alan started to stare at Merlin who was at the moment, resting on the cot on the other side of the room. He'd just started to scan Merlin when the entire structure they were in started to shake with a loud series of booms. Waving his hand Alan had a mirror appear in front of him showing him the exterior of the sanctuary. Counting Alan could see at least five of the dark mages out there. The funny thing though was that they all had an extremely mad look on their face. Staring harder at the mirror Alan spoke, "You five must feel awful brave to come here. I take it you wish to die today?"

"Alan Glanto! Get your ass out here this stops today! This is our world and ALL of these pitiful creatures are OUR slaves! Come out and face us and your end!" One who was obviously the leader and spokesman for the others shouted.

Sighing Alan walked to Hopix and kissed her passionately and deeply looking into her eyes, "I love you Hopix, I have for longer than I thought possible." Getting on a knee Hopix gasp, "I will return and we will unite as soon as this is done. I won't allow anything to come between us EVER! Wait for me my love!" With that he kissed her deeply again almost making her swoon. Then he was gone to the opening of the sanctuary.

Stepping out, Alan was surprised that they didn't attack him while he was climbing out. Though this changed the moment he hit the top of the stairs and moved away from the sanctuary entrance. Water, fire, electricity, and wind hit him from five different directions. Though he was almost at full power Alan still wasn't really feeling the effects of their attacks. Several yelled and increased their power, pushing his shields to the top of his power. Annoyed, Alan made a pronging motion at one of his attackers, who grabbed his throat choking then fell to the ground thrashing for a few seconds, then was still.

Undaunted the other four increased their power more, Alan hurled a bolt at another of the attackers literally frying him in his own blood as the second died gurgling his death rattle the others kept up their pressure on Alan. His face twisted in rage Alan's power elevated even higher as he sent several bolts of fire and electricity at the last three. Two of them were unprepared and dead before hitting the ground. The last snarled as Alan's attacks were reflected away.

"So the leader of the cowards is revealed!" Alan sneered at the semi-shaped man.

"Not cowards, comrades of the one you killed like a coward last night!" The leader growled out at Alan.

"That wasn't me I..." Alan started.

"You lie, you pathetic coward! I am here to exact vengeance on you!" The leader almost screamed at Alan. Again the leader started to hurl several attacks at Alan; hmmm not bad Alan thought the strongest I have faced except for the champion.

Sighing Alan decided the man wasn't going to listen and waited a few minutes the threw a few spells of his own at him. Screaming the man continued to fire at Alan pushing his power to the max Alan again hurled several more attacks at the man. This time almost all of them penetrated the man's defenses. With a surprised look and then a shrill scream the man was reduced to ash.

A great distance away, the champion had been watching, impressive, he thought, those had been low and middle, high-range mages. Alan had disposed of the first four as if they weren't there, what had the last done different? He also had to wonder how the white mage's power was increasing. At least to him it did. He always noticed everything it was the main reason he was still alive. He'd have to look into this before he face the man it just might prove an edge.

There were only thirty six of them left. Well, thirty five as one was the dark council's champion. The fact that they were freakishly strong compared to the rest that he had faced here wasn't lost on him either. Alan watched as the last of the ash or dust blew away the remnants of the last one of the five he had faced. Shaking his head he had to admit once they went evil, it obviously sucked all the intelligence out of them, really just how stupid could you get? Thinking you could defeat a far superior force even with help?

Thinking a moment more, Alan was really at a loss as to who was killing these mages; it wasn't the others, they might be bad, but they were fiercely loyal to each other and the council. There were only two white mages on the planet, and as far as he knew Merlin was still low level or was he? There really was something odd about the man, and Alan needed to get answers before this went any further.

Appearing back at the sanctuary, Alan decided that NOW was the time to talk to Merlin. Alan was a little surprised when he saw that Merlin was awake and waiting on him.

"I knew when I started this that you weren't stupid, I just thought it might take you a little longer to figure it out so that I had more time." Merlin told Alan with a heavy sigh.

"More time? More time for what?" Alan asked, an even more perplexed look on his face.

"More time to get my power higher, I have felt so useless for so long my power at such a low level. As you know, there are several levels of power. Those that are low just above apprentices, then the mid-range, a high range, then of course, there is what I have deemed an ultra-range. For many years I have tried to raise my power to be of more use, but alas failing each time. That is 'til I met you." Merlin explained.

"'Til you met me? What makes me so different from others?" Alan asked a look of concentration on his face.

"There are ways to grow ones power but as of yet I have not discovered any. You, my dear boy, can naturally increase your powers each time you use them. As I said there are those four levels each is divided into three parts of their own. When I first saw you, you were as high in the high range as you could go. You have since moved passed that into the ultra-range and I'd say that you are almost halfway through that now." Merlin went on.

"Alright, what has all this to do with your power?" Alan asked.

"Yes, right, I have always had an ability to ape or copy another's power if it was within my level. When you first released me I felt your power growing ability, at first I tried to copy it. After a few tries, I found it took all I had to do that. The most amazing thing I have found was that when I started to use my power again they started to grow! After I executed the first dark mage I felt my power move into the mid-range for the first time in my life. So, I kept practicing very, very slowly I built them up. After the second the other day, I discovered I was forming new abilities! I have never been able to thought move, now I can for several miles." Merlin had lowered his head.

"That explains why you slept so long it took a lot out of you I know that for a fact it always does. As the power increases so does the demand on the body 'til the body grows used to it." Alan told the man.

"I apologize for copying your power, I so desperately wish to return home to my Queen Glimmer, I have missed her so over the centuries. I am willing to do almost anything to make that happen, but I apologize to you, a fellow white mage." Merlin told Alan his head still bent low.

"I have seen your Queen Glimmer; I can understand, believe me, I would be the same way about Hopix as I love her with all my heart." Alan said as Merlin smiled funny, a gleam in his eye that wasn't lost on Alan.

Hopix had been in the great common room and was just returning when she heard Alan's confession about her to Merlin! Her mouth dropped open he loved her with all his heart!? She thought he was only just beginning to love her! Her heart soaring she stopped and just listened to the discussion as they went on.

"Merlin, I made a promise to your Queen Glimmer that I would find you and return with you. It is a promise I intend to keep, for now, I hold all the cards. I intend to keep it that way." Alan told a now shocked Merlin. "So tell me Merlin, just how high are your abilities now?"

"As I said I had already moved into the mid-range, and have been slowly building. The last I looked I was almost as high as I could go in the mid-range. The higher levels are taking much longer as I haven't given my body sufficient time to adjust, yet I was hoping that I could get high enough to actually aid you." Merlin explained sadly.

Alan had been nodding throughout Merlin's explanation, "We need to keep your levels a secret, and that means by everyone Hopix." Alan said with a smile, Hopix's head slowly eased around the doorway.

Her mouth hanging open Hopix was slowly advancing into the room. "But how...?" She started.

"As you heard my abilities have been increasing, lately I have tried to always know where you are. You mean far more to me than you at first thought." Here Alan smiled at Hopix giving her a warm feeling deep in her chest that she loved.

Turning back to Merlin Alan smiled, "I am sure just the fact that you can thought-move will be more than a little help. I am afraid that after these last five died, they won't come after me in mass anymore. We are going to have to go after them each separately. It might take a while they are the strongest and probably the smartest."

Merlin was shocked that Alan wasn't mad; had it been him he might have lost it feeling violated somewhat. Nodding his head, yes this man Alan was a rare find, looking over at Hopix he was definitely glad that he and she had finally gotten together. Then again Alan and she hadn't had sex yet, holy shit! Merlin smiled inside Alan was in for a real eye opener when that happened. Sex was one thing, but a Fairixie brought a whole new meaning to the phrase soul mate!

The little smiles Alan saw Merlin try to hide when he looked at him and Hopix wasn't lost on him either. There was a definite connection between a human and Fairixie that he had yet to realize. Soon he thought after this he and Hopix would be united. Alan felt that the type of union they were going to have was the type that many dreamed of but few ever found. Shaking his head, Alan decided help or not he needed to finish this, and soon, Hopix's body was beginning to drive him crazy the closer she was.

"I want you to stay here and work on your abilities; if and only IF you reach a higher level do I want you to even consider stepping out of this sanctuary. I mean it Merlin; I didn't come all this way just for you to get killed when I have almost cleared the planet." Alan told Merlin sternly.

Sighing Merlin nodded he might have higher power but as far as his body was concerned, he was still a weak mage trying to get by. "Alright, I'll try but this sitting here is killing me, I came here all those years ago to try and free this world. Alan they have a secret that you might find helpful later on. I was just starting to gain their confidence when I was betrayed!" Merlin growled a look of hurt on his face.

Nodding Alan and Hopix walked out and headed toward the surface, they needed to clear this planet soon. Alan could feel that the people were almost broken even those he'd freed were still in a vein of mind that this too would pass and they would be slaves again. Sighing all Alan could see was an almost repeat of the Tribocs it had taken the intervention of one of Queen Glimmer's people to open up their hearts enough for him to help them. He most definitely didn't want that to happen here.

Looking over at Hopix Alan nodded and they both made their way to the next or weakest of these left. Two sets of eyes watched as they left, one a soon to be great ally, another a great enemy only interested in the death of Alan and Hopix. They finally arrived at the place Alan guessed you would call it. Though to him it seemed as almost all of where the dark mages stayed were just dung heaps.

Firing off a few bolts Alan awaited the eventual screaming he knew would come. There was a rushing of power toward them then an almost ghostly apparition appeared in front of Alan, 'hmmmm this was different!'

"You dare to come here and insult me and my home? You are indeed as brash as the others said you were. No matter I have more than sufficient power to end your meddling here and now!" With that the apparition tried to surround him and take all the air from the space between it and Alan. Most definitely different! Finally, an enemy that was original and not the same old thing!

"As much as I am enjoying your company, I think it's time you left this world. I'll offer you the same deal as I did the others." Alan told the ghost like mage.

"It matters not! Within moments you will be

dead and then neither of us will have to worry about it!" The apparition told Alan.

Sighing and shaking his head Alan waved his hand and blew a hole in the wall that was in front of him. Screaming the ghost creature was trying to seal the hole when Alan told it, "Now about the deal. Just give up and leave, there will be no retaliation stay and well I'll have to kill you though I really don't want to."

The apparition stopped and stared at Alan, "You really don't know who you are up against with the dark council do you?"

Alan was shocked this was the first time a bad guy had actually stopped and talked, unlike so many.

"To surrender, to give up like you say may seem a simple thing to you but to all that now are in service to them it isn't. Many actually sign their lives to the council; to go against them says that they are free for the council to take. They actually OWN most of those that serve them, most not all. Even those they do not own are bound in some way to them. No matter what you say you can do, the dark council has a way to get past it and take all they are. So, when they say they can't or won't, they mean it." The ghost creature explained to him.

"Thank you, I guess I was being a little naive thinking I could turn them but it is a dream that I could at least save one." Alan told the creature a great sadness permeating his voice. Bowing to the creature Alan said, "I thank you are the first truly honorable one of the dark mages I have met."

A wicked smile crossed its face as several bolts

shot out of hiding behind Alan striking his shield. Nodding Alan's anger started to rise. Three of those behind him were suddenly fireballs of death each screaming in terror as they died. The fourth laughed wickedly as it bounced the spell back at Alan. Alan's eyes opened wide, hmmm, so they were finally starting to learn! Alan extended a hand and absorbed the spell that was flying toward him.

The wicked smile on the face of the fourth quickly faded, as it repositioned itself for better protection. The first had tried to flash out and found that it was effectively frozen to the spot it had appeared in. Alan smiled and waggled a finger at it then turned toward the fourth.

"You are the first to actually use your head. It is almost a shame to destroy you." Alan told the almost human-ant hybrid type creature. Again a wicked grin crossed its face as several almost appendage like, thick roots broke the ground below Alan latching onto his arms and legs.

Laughing wickedly, the fourth advanced upon Alan, with a smile of his own, Alan just nodded and broke the roots, then shot the fourth with several electric bolts. Screaming the dark mage had managed to erect a weak shield but it, like he, was dying rather quickly. Alan felt the first try to break free but Alan again waggled a finger at it without turning. Finally Alan pushed harder toward the fourth; finally the electrical bolts began to lick at the skin of it. Then there was the distinct smell of roasting flesh as the fourth was enveloped in the flames starting to erupt from where the bolts were touching the skin.

Growling Alan turned toward the first, "ALL OF YOU! EVERY ONE OF YOU!" Alan was yelling then calmed a moment, "I can finally feel the balance shifting on this world. Almost three fourths of the power that has held this world prisoner is gone. Once I have rid it of you I think the light council may be able to return here. I was going to give you a choice of how you died, but too bad!" A bolt shot from Alan's hands striking the first slowly part of it froze then crept up its body even slower. "You should be dead soon but I hope you enjoy this creeping freezing death good bye!"

Alan gathered Hopix and with a last look at the ghost apparition as a part of it broke off eliciting a scream, flashed out not far away. Concentrating, Alan had to be ready he could already feel the tens of thousands that were heading his way. Well he thought that was seventy of them, but I am afraid that the last thirty would be the worst, and then there was the champion.

Shaking his head Alan had already started to raise a large city this was going to be the biggest yet, he could feel upwards of one hundred thousand coming his way but then again just how many would actually want to be helped? An hour later the city had been finished and the first of those that would occupy it were starting to arrive. Having learned the last time Alan waited 'til there was a great number then shot out the same wave as before. Smiling he saw that all of these here truly wanted help.

Another two hours later, saw Alan starting to get frustrated, after the first ten or twenty thousand it had started to split fifty, fifty. Sighing now nine out of every ten didn't want the help The last bunch were approaching Alan was starting to grow tired he'd saved quite a few but there were so many left he had to develop a better way of doing this. At three hours he was finally finished of the one hundred five thousand that had appeared. Only seventy five thousand had accepted his help less than three fourths but still the greatest amount free on the planet in one place.

Alan and Hopix returned to the sanctuary, Alan took a step toward the door and started to fall; thankfully, Merlin was there and had managed to catch him before he was eating dirt. Inside Alan was laying on his pallet Hopix beside him unwilling to leave his side.

"I have felt the balance start to shift here," Merlin told him. "I believe that the Lobrits are feeling it also. You have done an extraordinary job Alan. I know you are tired, I know you want to go home with Hopix; we all have confidence in you. Always remember that there are far more for you than against you. Of the first three places you opened for the Lobrits, I feel those people are finally back to what they were. At the second they are almost there. The third you just finished they are already trying to set up government I feel the whole attitude of the people here is starting to change. Finally, the dream I had all those centuries ago is coming to fruition. Thank you Alan, thank you so much!"

Alan nodded, he was too tired after today to argue or ask questions, reaching over he gently caressed Hopix's face god he loved her! He had to finish this he had to, he'd waited all his life for a woman like Hopix and he wasn't about to lose her now! Alan kissed her hand as the fatigue finally took him and was asleep.

Merlin walked up to Alan extending his hands then nodded, Alan would be out completely for at least two hours, more than enough time to talk to Hopix.

"So when are you going to tell him?" Merlin asked a startled Hopix.

"Tell him? Whatever do you mean?" Hopix said feigning ignorance.

"Have you forgotten just who I am?" Merlin asked, "especially now with the increases that I have made?"

"No, I haven't forgotten, but it would be more than a distraction to him. He has felt so strong about this, that it is only a small thing to repay Glimmer and our planet. He has as strong a sense of duty as you do," Hopix told Merlin.

"I realize this, but child you have to tell him soon, especially with the two of you being joined soon. Don't you think he deserves to know? I know I would though in my case I would become exceedingly angry. I don't think this is the case for Alan." Merlin told her, staring at Hopix trying to gauge her reaction. Then he was shaking his head damn but these Fairixies were a hard race to read! It had taken well over 100 years to tell when his Glimmer had been joking or serious, rubbing his side he smiled that had been rough enough!

"You and he are so much the same and different, Queen Glimmer almost refused to allow him to come. He somehow convinced her, but I think she was thinking more of me than herself." Hopix told him.

Sighing Merlin nodded he knew his Glimmer all too well as she did him, were there was really no chance she would have tried with all she had to stop Alan. Looking at Alan with a new respect she had obviously seen something in the man that he hadn't, then again he'd seen some that he knew that Glimmer never would have.

"Alan is the first I found could do this job in a very long time. The fact that he loves me as I do him is of course an added bonus." Hopix added matter-of-factly.

"NO! It is far more than that and you know it damn it!" Merlin suddenly shouted then reigned in his emotions. "You have to tell him BEFORE your joining if you wait, I MAY have to tell him!" Merlin threatened.

"No please!" Hopix begged tears falling from her eyes. "I will tell him, but I am afraid that I will lose him when I do." Hopix said fresh tears falling anew from her eyes. "I cannot lose him." Hopix was whispering.

"My dear," Merlin told her, his voice softening, "if you don't tell him soon, you WILL lose him ok?" Hopix nodded she really hoped that Merlin was right she was so deeply in love with Alan she felt that if he rejected her she would quite literally die.

Merlin watched Hopix as she laid her head on Alan's chest he could feel the bond now, which meant he was finally into the higher range, Fat lot of good it did him now! Sighing he hadn't meant to upset Hopix, the truth needed to be known, especially with as strong a bond as they had. The same that he and Glimmer had thanked the stars he could still feel her and had all the time he was in the saving chamber.

It was a few hours later when Alan awoke, not opening his eyes he had a warm sensation on his chest. Opening one eye, he could just make out the top of Hopix's head on his chest, and then he felt the dampness. What the hell? What had happened that Hopix had been crying? Then he thought a moment that is if she had been crying he couldn't always tell with her. Looking around, he saw that Merlin was awake and staring at him.

[Can you hear me boy?] Alan heard Merlin in his head.

[Yes, but why are you thought talking?] Alan asked a little curious.

[I thought I might let her sleep she was awake for quite a while tending and watching over you,] came Merlin's reply.

[Ok, we'll let her sleep for now, thank you for your consideration.] Alan told Merlin.

[I wanted to ask what you are planning on doing. Only thirty of the dark mages are left before you face the champion. I am quite sure they all have laid a trap for you at one point or another.] Merlin advised Alan.

[Yes, I am well aware of that; then again I am betting that they think I will just walk into them too. I believe that they will be surprised when I appear to, but actually don't.] Alan replied.

Merlin smiled as he nodded he'd seen this young man's tactics, he was sure Alan had a few surprises up his sleeve. [I also wanted to tell you that I am as high as I can go in the mid-range. It is taking an untold amount of energy each time as you said. By the way I have felt a slight jump in your power as I said it is extremely slow. After the mid-range I am having a difficult time increasing.]

[Just remember it takes a little bit for your body to adjust before you should even think of trying to go further. What I did today was the largest I have ever done, the sleep helped greatly but I don't think I want to push it like that again for a bit.] Alan explained.

[Yes, I know, I have slowed trying to increase, the amount of energy as you said, is enormous. Please, Alan be careful these last thirty are the worst of the lot.] Merlin warned.

Alan nodded, reached down, and gently kissed Hopix, sending shivers up his spine. Withdrawing his lips he could see that Hopix was feeling it as well. "Hello, my love; feeling better?" Alan asked when her eyes flew open.

Breathing hard, Hopix could only nod as she clung to Alan as if her life depended on it.

"We need to get started; I feel it won't take too many more before the light council will be able to appear on this world. You sure you feel like going with me?" Alan asked a smile on his face as a sudden look of anger crossed Hopix's face.

"You wouldn't dare think of leaving without me!" She told him as she playfully slapped his shoulder.

Alan nodded, then arose with Hopix's arms still around him. "I want to finish this as fast as possible but I think that the last thirty are counting on me being reckless."

"I believe you are right; maybe a calming meditation," Hopix asked, to which Alan could only stare at her. To him meditation with his wife was when she actually left him alone!

Taking a deep breath Alan sighed, and then shrugged hell it couldn't hurt to try now could it. Concentrating on Hopix's face Alan could actually feel the tension leave his body; amazing! Then a new idea started to form, hmmm Alan thought a little devious but it might work.

Half an hour later, Alan and Hopix were leaving the sanctuary, Alan feeling for the next mage he was going after. Nodding to Hopix they started to head in that direction as fast as possible. Finally, they arrived at a ... tree? Shaking his head Alan knew they were weird guess he should expect it. Smiling then nodding to Hopix, Alan raised his power and cut the top of the tree off. As he expected there was a large amount of screaming before the mage appeared.

"You bastard how dare you destroy my home! I will use your bones in the construction of my next home!" Firing a (here Alan just shook his head) huge fireball at Alan the half bird shaped mage started to laugh. "I know you have a superior defense against fire but this is quite different!"

Alan just nodded he'd felt the more intense heat but it was really nothing to him. Bouncing it back Alan watched as the dark mage's face showed surprise as it extended its arm like appendages. Suddenly the face twisted into fear and hate as the fire ball didn't extinguish but built to a higher intensity. Alan suddenly was speaking to the air as he stated, "I hope all of you are watching, I am through playing with you whether now or later, alone or together. I am coming to end each of you do us all a favor and just give up! None of you have a chance, NONE of you!"

Turning away Alan smiled, 'That ought to do it, ' he thought. Looking at the bird creature mage Alan pushed some more, feeling the other lose the fight. Finally, amidst an increasing amount of screaming as it died, several more dark mages appeared and started to fire different attacks at Alan. Many of the new arrivals' faces twisted into hate as they all tried to end Alan at the same time.

Smiling Alan had felt the approach of the ten that were now striking at his shields. Alan had depended on the fact that most of them were conceited about their power, good he thought as he slowly increased his shields and then started to push back. Hmmm, Alan thought as he felt the familiar presence of the dark council's champion. Turning his attention back to the new arrivals, Alan made several different cutting motions as four of the new mages fell bleeding from gashes on their throats and necks.

Several of those left started to push harder growling out their hatred of Alan. Increasing his power even more Alan was almost as high as he'd been before pushing back hard as another two screamed. Their own attacks caught and consumed them as they died beside the others. Ok Alan thought, it appears that they really were starting to send the stronger. 'It was about time, ' he thought, 'this would definitely be a challenge!'

Still, the first that Alan had engaged was trying to escape, again waggling his finger at him. Alan thought I ought to try something different. Concentrating, Alan could feel the ground beneath him and the dark mages; smiling he reached down, and a moment later three of the four left, screamed. Several roots erupted from the ground and ripped them apart, the last only smiled as he pointed a stubby finger-like appendage at Alan.

"So, mage Alan you can learn! Good it will make this victory over you that much sweeter!" With that the last mage faded to a mist that floated toward Alan, an evil cackling emitting from it. "You can stop most attacks but not this one! Remember how brave you thought you were when you feel your lungs on fire and you blood boiling out of your body!"

Alan could only smile he'd seen something like this before and awaited the approach of the dark mage. As it drew closer Alan's grin got bigger making the mist falter a moment; that was all Alan needed as a freezing wave of cold erupted from Alan. Screaming the mist tried to avoid the cold and almost made it.

"I would say it had been a good fight but you were rather easy," Alan told the half frozen mist. "It's a shame you have been the most original yet, oh well." Stepping forward Alan brought a foot down on the frozen section of the mist effectively shattering it into thousands of pieces. Screaming the dark mage cursed at Alan then stopped as it died.

Turning back to the first of the dark mages Alan got a curious grin on his face. The first of Alan's assailant's eyes got wide then it looked behind Alan and started to grin.

"I see that my true help is here!" Quite confident the first dark mage started to laugh at Alan. "Soon you will be dead, and we all will profit handsomely!"

Behind Alan a now familiar voice broke the air, "I know you aren't talking about me! You are a stupid and pathetic fool to think I would help a weak idiot like you in fact." Suddenly there was a massive build up of power then a rushing release that shot out and engulfed the creature. Screaming it was gone quicker than Alan thought it would be. "I cannot stand the weak and sniveling fools the council has working for them. That though, is their business I could care less."

"Huh and here I thought you had no honor," Alan told the dark council's champion.

"Oh, rest assured I do not! Though when it comes to you who can know? You are mine to kill, the sooner these impossible wastes are gone, the sooner I can feast on your soul!" The powerful dark mage said. "I won't kill them; that is your job as is dying at the appointed hour by my hand. So do us all a favor, kill them quickly I thirst for an actual battle against a real mage not." HE kicked what was left of the first dark mages body. "These wastes of space." Laughing evilly the creature disappeared.

Alan shook his head then sat to rest a few minutes, he could already feel a huge multitude coming this way. There had to be a way to speed up the process. "Hopix, do you think there is an easier way to complete the clearing of these people?"

Sitting next to him her chin on her hand she also started to think, a few minutes later she looked at Alan excited. "Alan, do they have to be awake for you to actually do this? I have seen that the more they struggle before you actually stop working on them, the more energy you use. Perhaps it would be simpler to just put them asleep?"

Alan sat there mulling over what she'd said, maybe she was right it took a lot more energy to fight them trying to open them up awake then when they were asleep. The last group he'd worked on had been this way hell, it was worth a shot! Wiping out the home of the first dark mage Alan set about making a major city comparable to one that he'd seen in the minds of many of the Lobrits. He'd just finished when he felt the overly large throng of Lobrits as they drew close.

"I know that most of you are confused, I have created a city for you, but first, I need you to sleep." At this all that were there dropped to the ground in slumber. Alan started on the first few thousand finding it three times easier than he thought it would have been. Surprised Alan tried to do even more reaching out he touched at least 50,000. Smiling he found it was a hell of a lot easier plus he hardly felt the strain that he had before.

An hour later, Alan could only guess that he'd had well over two hundred thousand there though this time he was surprised that only about ten thousand didn't want to be free. Shaking his head he sent all that were free now into the city and set up all the protection. Sighing he still couldn't believe that many chose to remain with their dark mage masters.

Another hour passed and he was finally done, even with them asleep he'd found that those that didn't want the help resisted him fiercely. Then he thought about what the dark council champion had said, shaking his head he could almost sense the excitement that the other had about facing him. Was the man, (Alan guessed he had been at one time) really that much in love with fighting as Alan could feel? Alan had just turned to Hopix when he felt a familiar presence appear.

"I thought you were going to wait 'til your power had increased more," Alan asked of Merlin.

"I'm not sure, if you can tell," Merlin replied. "I was practicing again when I felt something slip and I suddenly knew that I had increased into the higher range. I am nowhere by far even close to you but I am feeling a hell of a lot more confidence than I was." Here Merlin waved his arm with a small flourish sending a small shower of sparks out from his arm. "I have never been able to do that before, neither have I been able to thought move as far as I have." Leaning close Merlin told a now shocked Alan in a whisper, "I made it here in two moves."

"What!? You'd have to move into... ," Alan started to smile, so the old man had finally moved into the higher ranges. Well Alan thought now the man was in for it that was for sure, the last nineteen might think he WAS an easier target but now Ha! Alan could only imagine all of their surprised faces when they went after him now.

Merlin smiled when he could see that Alan had the same revelation that he'd had. Then he remembered the real reason he'd come there, "I came as fast as I could, the first small town you created is under attack from those that chose not to be freed. They had contacted me as you were gone, I have tried to add more protection to the outer walls, but I am afraid I haven't near the power you do."

Alan nodded he'd felt tremors from the protection he'd erected but nothing all that serious yet. Then again with the strongest left that might change quickly. "I'll head there as soon as we are done here," Alan told a worried Merlin.

Merlin could only nod, he wanted these people free they, reminded him of a few of the kinder races he'd met. He just hoped that Alan wasn't too late, this attack had been different than most that he'd felt before, another shock to him that he was feeling more. Merlin nodded to Hopix with a reproachful look as he concentrated and vanished.

Alan checked all of the safeguards he'd put in place then gathered up Hopix, and they both vanished. Appearing not far from the first place Alan had set up for the Lobrits, Alan quickly assessed the situation. Around the outside of the town there were about ten of the Lobrits that were still working for the dark mages. Each had their arms raised and emitting various energy towards the shields that Alan had erected around the town.

Growling Alan could feel the presence of at least three of the stronger dark mages through the ten of the loyal Lobrits. Alan was approaching when he heard a voice, "Hold mage Alan! Under the rules of conquest, those in this pathetic village are ours!"

Alan sneered yelling, "Then they are all mine! I

defeated all of those before me, release them, and halt this attack! I suggest you do so before you truly piss me off!"

"As if there was anything you could do!" The voice yelled back as several of the servant Lobrits turned toward Alan and started firing.

Alan smirked and easily blocked the attack even as several more bolts shot toward him from behind. Hopix screamed a warning as all three of the bolts started to penetrate his shields. Damn it! Distracted only a moment Alan returned fire catching the first of the three mages igniting its skin. Amid the screams, the last two poured on more power, finally breaking through, one barely grazing Alan's arm. Grimacing Alan's now almost useless arm fell at his side. Looking at Hopix's furious face as she helped him to remain standing Alan concentrated and they vanished.

They only managed to go a few thousand yards, both of the dark mages decided to give chase. Again Alan tried to move them but the pain was starting to distract him, as again they only moved a few thousand yards. Finally clear of the town Alan and Hopix looked at his arm, though not as bad as the first time he'd been injured it was more painful. Alan was about to move again when Merlin appeared.

"I thought you were in trouble something had felt off when I felt your first move" Alan could barely nod as the pain racked his body almost to the point that he was fighting to stay conscious. "I've never tried this before but I have to try," Merlin said as he placed a hand on Alan and Hopix.

More than half way to the sanctuary Merlin and his passengers appeared startled Merlin recognized where they were. Shaking his head he could suddenly feel both of the following mages but they were at an extreme distance, damn had they moved that far? Closing his eyes Merlin concentrated on the sanctuary and they vanished again appearing outside the front of the sanctuary. Again Merlin's eyes grew large this was amazing! This was fantastic! This was, shit! Merlin could feel the drain on his body and power well he thought as he started to fall this sucks!

Hopix's eyes were wide when had Merlin's power increased that much? Merlin had never shown this much power the whole time they had been here! There was a sudden commotion as the Lobrits came pouring out of the sanctuary to carry not only Alan but a now unconscious Merlin inside.

The dark champion was shaking his head maybe he'd given this mage Alan far too much credit to be hurt by such a tactic. Then again it was really the first time such had been used against him, we'll see he thought Alan learned a hell of a lot faster than he was used to, Maybe this was a ruse? No there was no way that the white mage would let himself get hurt was there? Obviously, there was a lot more to this Alan than met the eye. Yes further study was required that was for sure before they faced off against each other. With a smug and extremely confident look, the dark champion vanished, already forming plans of ways to defeat Alan.

They managed to get Alan inside without incident as well as Merlin; that was 'til they set Alan down, and the pain shot through his body. Doing his best not to scream Alan lay there as several healers started to work on him. Damn, Alan thought he couldn't even feel them at first, then slowly, he started to feel a tiny bit of the pain fade.

They had been at it for perhaps four hours when Alan heard Merlin stir with a groan. Hopix had also added her power to the healing, but it appeared that even her power was far insufficient to do all that much to his injuries. Merlin's eyes opened, 'damn, ' he thought as the room spun, 'I'm a little surprised I am awake.' Looking over at Alan he could see that Alan's arm was still in bad shape. Barely able to move Merlin directed some of his energy toward Alan, watching as it enveloped the arm. Alan's eyes snapped open as he actually felt his arm healing. 'Who the hell was that, ' he thought there was no one powerful enough...

Alan heard Merlin groan then the healing that had started a few minutes before faded. Alan tried to move his arm not great but it was by far better than it had been. Looking at Merlin, the man smiled then promptly passed out, damn Alan thought the man really had advanced his power that far! Concentrating Alan could finally add to the healing as he felt the tender flesh become whole. Alan's last thought as the healing had also drained him was he had to repay the man when they were both awake, well after the last seventeen mages, and the champion were gone.

CHAPTER 3

Alan awoke, startled at first as he didn't recognize exactly where he was. Then he felt a soft body next to his looking down he saw that Hopix had at some time climbed into the bed with him for warmth. God Alan thought she feels so good so soft so...! Alan had looked under the covers, growing hard as he found that Hopix was stark naked! Holy shit he thought as he could only stare at her naked form my god! She's perfect!

Slowly Alan reached under the covers and began to gently massage the outer section of Hopix's breast that was crushed up against him. God! Alan thought she had felt soft before but this! I am going to go insane if this keeps up Alan thought I need to finish with this so Hopix and I can be alone for a while.

Merlin was doing his best not to make a sound, he remembered the first time he'd seen and been with his Glimmer. The woman completely blew away the things he thought he knew about love. Then Merlin felt the deep emptiness that was in his heart, though he could feel her he was still longing to hold her again. Merlin could feel that his power had grown again but I really shouldn't try something like that again unless I have no choice he thought.

Reaching out Merlin could suddenly feel a myriad of different life forms on the planet, what the hell? This was something entirely new to him and though it was a good thing it could drive one mad if he didn't get a handle on it. Merlin hadn't measured his power in a while, the last he knew it was at the fringe of the high power. Feeling again Merlin saw that yes, he was into the high range but still at the far low end of it.

Alan was enjoying the soft sighs and pressing of Hopix's body to him when he too noticed that Merlin was reaching out. "Merlin," Alan whispered to the man. "You have to learn to tune it out, or it will always be on but you can turn it down 'til you hardly notice it at all."

Merlin looked at Alan then nodded trying Alan's suggestion, to his surprised it worked! Well for a few minutes, and then he had to reapply the tune down. Thankfully it was lasting longer each time.

"Alan love that feels so good, please don't stop!" Hopix suddenly whispered to Alan.

"Hello beautiful, though I see you are in your full glory already. Why may I ask are you undressed?" Alan said with a smile to Hopix.

"Well, you started to shiver last night so I thought to give you warmth. Besides I was getting cold myself. I hope you don't mind but I couldn't have you getting sick." Hopix told Alan calmly and matter of factly.

"Ok I agree with that but why my dear are you undressed? Alan asked her again.

"Well," Hopix started, "we are to be wed and you

have seen me undressed before, so I thought it would be ok with you to add more warmth without my clothes."

Alan sighed and tried to make himself more comfortable, damn he thought I thought Glimmer had talked to her. Alan looked at the beautiful woman lying pressed against him, leaned down, and whispered into her ear.

Hopix lay still as Alan whispered in her ear, and then she reached down Alan's body and felt his hardness. Suddenly red faced she kissed Alan and was clothed, leaning back she told him, "I had forgotten my soon to be husband." Pausing a moment she looked under the cover then smiled at him. "I won't again; never will I forget the gifts you have given me." Leaning closer she whispered, "Plus those that you will give me. I will do all I can to be your partner my love," kissing him she leaned closer emphasizing, "ALL I can."

Alan could only stare at Hopix as she got up on shaky legs then walked to the common room. Merlin had a huge smile on his face, ah the young in love!

Alan wasn't sure exactly what the hell had just happened but he loved it! His whole body was tingling as was his very hard male anatomy! Sighing Alan didn't want to get up but knew that seventeen bad mages out there wanted his soul. The really bad thing though was these wouldn't just roll over and die as easily as the others had. Shit Alan thought I really got my work cut out for me.

Alan got up finally, as did Merlin, "I see that you have finally moved into the third stage of power. Be careful Merlin, when I moved into it, the creeps seemed to come out of the wood work!"

"I am well aware Alan, I may not have been able to move, but I was watching. You have achieved quite a lot in a fairly short time. The simple fact that you freed both of the, what is it you call them? Ah! Yes! The Fairixies, the fact that you have freed both of their worlds is nothing short of a miracle. I never did get a chance to thank you for freeing my Glimmer and her people." Here Merlin bowed to Alan who was really uncomfortable.

"Look, I am not a god ok? I am a man like you well kind of like you. I only do these things because they are right that's all, ok?" Alan told an even wider smiling Merlin.

"Yes son I know. Remember this though; you have freed worlds that have been slaves for centuries in less than six months. You are the first that has had enough power to do that. No! You are more special than you think, but I am glad that you are doing all this for the reasons you are. Now then we need to discuss what you are going to do next, I know I am not a lot of help but I will be there if you need me. Believe me Alan I owe you far more than you think and I hope that one day you can truly appreciate just what you have done for me."

Alan was taken aback he wasn't used to really any praise at all but the amount of praise the old man was giving him was making him really, really uncomfortable! "I have to defeat at least one more then I feel that the light council will be able to appear here," Alan told Merlin.

Merlin was nodding he felt that also, and then realized with a shock that it had just come to him that he had the knowledge. "Yes I have felt that also but these last few aren't going to be that easy."

"I know that's why I thought..." with that Alan launched into his newly formed plan.

Merlin's eyes opened wide it was a bold plan, dangerous and a little risky but it could work they just needed a little luck.

Later that day, Alan was standing outside what appeared to be a burned tree but wasn't sure. Shrugging Alan paused a moment and released a blast at about half his power. There he thought that ought to wake up the stupid ass! Sure enough, several bolts of electricity shot out of the sky a few moments later at Alan. Smiling Alan watched as they harmlessly bounced off his shields.

A voice behind Alan made him sigh, the same old thing damn! These guys, as powerful and old as they are, didn't seem to have any idea of the pain Alan would bring upon them. Sighing Alan waited as the being he guessed was part snail with huge human eyes appeared. Then of course it started to boast, yawning Alan just stood there and tuned out. A few moments later the creature stopped with a growl.

"So you think to disrespect me this way? I am far more powerful than you think I will..." Alan finally tired of it waved his hand and the creature was silent.

"Finally, so here's how it's going to go, first I'm going to freeze you," with that Alan waved another hand and the creature stopped moving. "Then I'm just going to kill you. Good bye!" Alan let loose a titanic burst of energy that enveloped the creature, and it was suddenly gone.

Alan waved his hand and looked at a small sphere that formed in front of him. "I am tired of you cowards hiding but if you want to die that way so be it." Pointing at the sphere a misshapen deer like animal appeared in front of him. "Now then that's better!" Alan made a slashing motion, and the creature was dead that quick. Well that's two Alan thought, but I won't be able to get the rest as easily.

Alan suddenly heard a clapping behind him, "God I'm glad you are as smart as you are! If you went about it any other way I might have killed you out of boredom. Now I see you truly will be a challenge after all!" Alan felt the huge fireball as it approached him. He was ready this time and easily bounced back at the man. Though expecting something of this nature the man was surprised that Alan had done it as easily as he had. Hmmm, the man thought so maybe he was pretending the other day. Yes, I'll have to watch him closely. Then the man saluted Alan and was gone.

Damn it! Alan thought he had hoped that the bastard would have been hurt. Turning back to the sphere Alan pointed at it again as another winged snake like creature appeared, though startled it attacked almost immediately. Alan smiled so they were smarter after all, as long as he had control of the sphere he could draw almost all of them here but the sphere was limited. Making several slashing motions this one fell as had the others.

Alan had to hurry he could feel the sphere growing weak, pointing three times Alan knew that this was risky but he had to do it. Suddenly there was a loud screaming as the first appeared. The second hissed a warning, and the third just started to fire at Alan. Smiling Alan hoped they were using their full power as he started to bounce their attacks back at one other than who fired it. The screams he heard let him know it was working as already one was down.

Alan attacked the weakest of the two hoping this worked he surrounded the creature with a cloud. Within a minute, the cloud lifted, and the creature was dead.

"So wanna give up before I kill you?" Alan shouted at the last one.

"Kiss my wart covered ass you repulsive human! After I kill you I think I'll keep your head as a trophy." The huge toad like creature said as it started to laugh and spit venom at Alan.

Well, Alan thought that's original! Let's see how he likes the taste. Alan made a covering motion with his hand as the toad creature kept trying to spit at him. Too late it realized its mistake as its stomach grew larger then exploded! Alan had already moved a distance away. Looking at the sphere Alan thought he might get one more when it winked out.

Alan thought that's six less, but how hard will the last eleven be? The champion had been watching from a distance, the porta sphere had been brilliant! A direct path to those viewing it, unable to look away or disconnect truly a stroke of genius! The champion was starting to get more excited this was going to be a battle that he would savior the rest of his life!

Alan was pissed he'd hated using that, having

learned it not long ago. There was another trick he could use but he felt he needed another day at least before he could even think of using it. Hmmm Alan thought maybe Merlin had a few tricks he hadn't thought of after all Merlin had been doing this with less power for a lot longer and had survived.

Alan was about to go when he felt that the sphere was still there just weak, he had to try one more time. Concentrating Alan pointed four times; this could kill me he thought. A few moments later four extremely pissed off shapes; a snake, an ogre, a beetle, and a bent and broken looking man appeared in front of him. I have to move quickly Alan thought as he made a slashing motion a few times. Two of those in front of him stopped and keeled over.

"Weak fools! You may have gotten us here, but you will never end u..." The one that had been speaking suddenly couldn't say anything as blood gushed from its mouth. With a startled look it gagged and fell over.

The misshapen and broken looking human smiled at Alan. "Very good, or lucky," it said as the face twisted into a horrid mask of hatred. Alan nodded; this one wasn't going to be fooled like the others. His defenses were high and in place. They were wrapped tight like a bl... , Alan suddenly smiled he had him beat.

The warped man moved in trying to gain an advantage when he found he couldn't move! What the hell was going on? That's when he saw that Alan was bending his wrapped shields onto him. Shit! He was going to die from his own protection! Releasing his shields Alan was ready as he fried the last dark mage with a barrage of electrical attacks.

Laughing as he was dying the last dark mage told Alan, "Enjoy this victory; you won't beat my brother, you dog of the council!"

Alan reached out to make sure that the sphere was indeed gone. That was nine of the last seventeen, it had taxed him to a point that he tried not to reach. Shit Alan thought I need to get back, thinking of the sanctuary he'd moved maybe a thousand yards. Oh crap Alan thought as he felt his reserves start to dwindle.

Merlin and Hopix appeared a moment later, grabbed him and were back at the sanctuary in less than a minute. Merlin's eyes opened wide damn! That was the longest and furthest he'd ever moved not bad, aw shit! Merlin slightly stumbled as they took Alan into the sanctuary. "Thank you Merlin," Alan slurred, then collapsed on his bed.

Merlin nodded then almost fell his self his power was growing but so was the demand on his body. Damn it! They still had eight out there and they were going to be the toughest of them all. I sure hope Alan is up for them his power was in the ultra-level but it hadn't moved much at all. Hell from what he felt Alan was still only half way through the ultra-level. Hopix walked to Merlin and hugged him. "Thank you, thank you for helping me save him. I was afraid that he'd gotten himself killed going alone."

Hopix turned back to Merlin then smiled as he too was now passed out though, he hadn't quite made it to his cot. Shaking her head, she didn't know what she was going to do with either of them, the most important men in her life besides her brother.

Sighing she decided that it must be a trait of all men from earth, to jeopardize their lives worrying the women that loved them.

Alan was floating in a gray area, this was much like the dream world I was in before, he thought. Reaching out Alan started to smile ah! He could see it wasn't from him, this was from somewhere else. A few moments later the figure of Hopix appeared before him.

"Hello Alan," she told him, "I have missed you, come back to me so we can be together." Reaching out the vision tried to wrap its arms around Alan but he pushed her away. "What is wrong my Alan? I have wanted you for so long I know that you will fulfill me more than any other. Come to me now my love!"

Alan was shaking his head it was a good ruse, if they had a lot better information than they did. "Very convincing are you really a man or are you one of the rare ones that once was a female?" The vision of Hopix's eyes went wide but whoever it was kept in character well.

"My love why do you say these hateful things to me? I love you! I want..." The visage of Hopix was saying.

"Look, drop it ok? I already know you aren't her, so drop it! Maybe I should just blow you away!" Alan said as he watched his hands start to glow then just as suddenly go dark.

The Hopix vision started to laugh then the voice started to change, getting higher and a hell of a lot more irritating. As he watched, the vision of Hopix started to bend and twist 'til it was misshapen. Alan could swear the meat was falling off the bones, the hair what little was left was stringy, greasy with a horrid odor that was filling the air. Sighing Alan had expected no less.

Wait a minute! He could smell the odor of her hair. Smiling he knew where they were now. "As you can see you have no power here but I am all powerful. Bah I don't know why I'm telling you!" Finally Alan thought one who used their head!

Alan watched as the twisted female shape rushed toward him, drawing a hand up from his side he heard her gasp! "You really thought I wouldn't figure it out? Please! I might be new to this but I'm not stupid!" Alan stood stock still he only had two chances at this as they were still locked into her alternate reality.

The woman was starting to back away as Alan's hands were starting to get brighter. "No! You are locked in this realm with me MY realm, there is no way you could access your power unless..."

The woman stopped short, realizing that Alan was using life energy, though a moment too late as Alan blew half her body away. On the other side of the planet, the woman's real body began to jerk and convulse. two others watched as her eyes and ears started to bleed, and she began to vomit up blood.

Back in the alternate reality, Alan could see that she was finished he'd felt almost half his power flow back in. Quickly Alan drew in all he could, "I should kill you just on the principle of you trying to disgrace Hopix, but ah hell, just DIE!" Alan released another blast nearly as big as the last, this time he took what was left of the top of her body.

In the woman's home the other two were shaking their head it had been foolish to think the white mage would have been fooled. Then the now dead woman's body sat up and looked directly at them. "When I started today there were seventeen, then eleven, that was whittled to eight. I don't know whose idea this was I don't care who's idea this was. Suffice it to say that before, I was doing this because it was right. Try something like that again, and I will make your deaths truly painful." With that the body dropped, broken and empty both of the dark mages looked at each other than vanished.

Merlin awoke not too long after he'd fainted still weak he tried to bring something to drink to himself when he noticed Alan glowing. What in the hell was going on? He hadn't seen anything like this since Morgan le Fay was learning every scrap of magic she could. As he'd told Alan he'd never been very powerful but had developed tricks that truly deceived all who saw them. Hell, they even fooled Morgan le Fay 'til the day she tried to kill him.

Merlin stretched out his feelings and hit a damn hard thick wall! What the hell was going on? Pushing harder Merlin could finally hear Alan but still couldn't see anything. Trying one more time, Merlin was finally through in a sense, though they couldn't hear him. Merlin watched with pride as Alan took the other out almost with ease. Retreating Merlin was afraid he'd be trapped there if he didn't.

Alan awoke with a start that was an experience, looking at Merlin; Alan could see he was still fast asleep. Back in the home of the female mage the champion just shook his head. What a fool he thought, the white mage was new true, but he wasn't as unknowledgeable as most of them thought.

Alan could hear Hopix calling him, damn, she was so far away! Alan started to claw his way to the surface, fighting with every fiber of his being. Finally, he opened his eyes seeing a look of love and worry on Hopix's face.

"Alan my love you need to drink this, you are far too weak, please, my love." Hopix held a cup with a foul smelling brew in it. [I've smelled that before,] Alan thought, [when was it? Ah yes back when he'd been on the Fairixie's sister world.] Alan tried to drink it as fast as he could; again not realizing that one couldn't swallow the concoction as fast as he was trying. Coughing and sputtering Alan was gasping for breath as the foul odor of it surrounded him.

Barely in a whisper, had Alan told Hopix, "My god woman, it's still as bad as it was before!" Hopix smiled, Alan complaining meant that the brew was already coursing through his body helping to strengthen it.

"Alan, please don't go off alone like that again. I was assigned to help you because you might have a lot of knowledge, but you don't know it all." Hopix admonished him her slender hand on her hip as she gently wiped the excess from his mouth.

Again starting in a whisper but growing stronger Alan told her, "Hopix my love I realize this, but you have to realize that if I was to lose you I might go insane, or worse kill everything in my way 'til I calmed. I do not want to put you in harm's way like that."

"Alan Glanto! If you weren't as weak as you were right now, I might have to, as you humans say on your planet, kick your ass!" Alan could swear there was steam coming from Hopix's ears.

Holding his arms and hands up in protection, Alan didn't doubt she could kick his ass! There was no way that he could ever hurt her. "My love, I was only thinking of protecting you, I..." Alan started.

Hopix stood up with now both her hands on her hips a look of anger that actually had Alan shaking. "I was YOUR guardian BEFORE you became as powerful as you have. I am a lot older than you, I have been dealing with dark mages far longer than you think. Shut me out of doing MY JOB again, and YOU will find out just how weak I am NOT!" Alan was staring at Hopix a new respect for her in his eyes.

"I promise you I will never exclude you again, my dear." Alan told her a slight smile on his face. "You can stop right now, old man I am sure Glimmer will have quite an earful for you when we return."

Merlin had tried not to, truly he had, but he'd finally started to laugh. It was hard to tell who was the more fierce Hopix or Alan, though it appeared to be Hopix at the moment.

Hopix turned and stared coldly at Merlin, who started laughing even harder. "I will deal with the both of you later!" Hopix growled as she marched out of the room.

"To answer your question, Glimmer was that fierce, always in her love, her compassion, and her temper. I am surprised this is the first time you have seen it, at least you know what to expect. I was caught off guard the first time after I was married to Glimmer." Merlin told Alan, who was watching as Hopix's form retreated into the other room.

"I have to ask you Merlin you have survived a long time with little or no power. I used the porta sphere to get nine of the last seventeen. I also got one that was trying to draw me to another reality; that leaves seven. I am afraid that these last seven won't band together nor attack when another is fighting me. With all the tricks you have, I need help getting them. I want this over, so I can take you and Hopix back home to the Fairixie world." Alan told Merlin, feeling he was almost at the end of his rope with these idiots on this world.

"I do have a few tricks, but I think I need a few things for you to learn. But the way you are right now, almost the entire planet can feel you coming. I think that is where we need to start; then I can possibly help you with a few things that might help." Merlin smiled it had been a long time since he'd had anything like a student it felt good, damn good!

Alan gave an exasperated yell as he'd failed again to do exactly what Merlin had shown him. "Damn it, Merlin I have been full tilt the whole time I have been doing this. How in the hell do you expect me to tune it down?"

"Son, I am into the high levels now and I can do this, so I know it's possible. Here's something that might help. Take a deep breath and as you let it out, feel the power decrease in you, that's it another breath let your body relax let all the tension flow out of you. As you do this you'll feel your power levels start to drop, and there you go well. See? It wasn't that hard now was it? " Merlin told Alan with a huge smile.

Alan's eyes snapped open his levels were so low it was unreal; staying as calm as he could Alan could feel his levels even out but they stayed low. "This is amazing I never thought I could make them this low."

"Well to you they're low, to me they are in the mid-range, but you are getting there. Compared to where you really are this is a major accomplishment. Now then let's work on a few more before we rest ok?" Alan nodded he was extremely glad he'd asked Merlin to help.

Two days later, across the planet, two of the remaining seven dark mages received a summons to the home of a third. The third was an ally of the first two and had mentioned a plan to destroy the white mage that couldn't fail. When the third mention a meal of a Fairixie; namely the one with the white mage they jumped at the chance.

Outside what could only be described as a murky swamp with a tumbling down shack in the middle the two dark mages appeared?"Trigafor! We are here! Where is this meal that you promised us?" The taller of the two called reaching out he could feel the third but something strange was going on. Neither felt any other mage or power anywhere near; suddenly Alan appeared with Merlin and Hopix.

"So, I see you came as I asked," Alan told them as they both discovered that they couldn't leave let alone move. Alan waved his hand and the third appeared a look of extreme anger on its face.

"You are an ass white mage! Release me! I will

eat all of your soul before..." Alan sighed and clapped his hands as the third screamed and was a mashed puddle of flesh, blood, and bone. Alan was turning toward the first two when one broke free of the spell holding him.

"Not so fucking powerful, are you bitch?" The one that got lose snarled shooting a freeze spell of his own that hit Alan in his left arm. Cursing when the Tall putrid, smelling human shape dark mage started to laugh, Alan quickly shot another paralyzing spell toward it. Laughing again the dark mage side stepped the spell. Smiling, Alan increased his shield then shot more spells toward the dark mage. "Damn! Here I thought you were this all powerful white mage!"

Alan started to smile even bigger, making the dark mage angry, shaking his head, Alan watched as his first three spells returned. Outraged the dark mage stopped a moment, then whipped around just as the first spell froze him solid. Alan breathed a sigh of relief as the next shattered the frozen form.

The last struggled, also breaking free though this time Alan was ready and fried the dark mage as he was making a move toward Alan. Alan shook his arm as he felt the feeling start to return to it.

"Nice move getting hit to fake the idiot out!" The now familiar voice of the dark council champion could be heard behind Alan. "I am so ready to fight you! Hurry up and kill the last four, then, I can have an actual battle with a worthy opponent. Here is something to keep you warm." With that, the champion left and sent a fireball at least twelve feet high toward Alan.

Alan felt this was different so he sent Merlin and Hopix a little ways off. Erecting a magical water barrier, Alan knew it wasn't enough but it would weaken it enough for him to squash it. As he thought the barrier cut it by half, it moved his way again. Alan slapped his hands together, and the fireball hesitated, still trying to reach him. Alan put more and more into it 'til he was as high as he could go, he felt the fireball falter and flame out.

Damn, Alan thought that was exhausting, there was a sudden rush of air, and then the light council was there before him. "You have done a most wonderful job Alan, of the 100 dark mages and well over 300 apprentices that were here. There are only four dark mages left. Know this, Alan though we can now come and go from here freely we still cannot interfere. We are sorry but as per the rules that were set down by both you and the dark council, this is all we can do. You should also know that this is all the dark council can also do." Alan nodded to the leader of the light council then they were gone.

Both Hopix and Merlin appeared a moment later; Merlin had wanted nothing to do with the council, especially now that he had as much power as he did. "I want to thank you both for coming with me; I think I should go after another if you two are up for it?" Alan told them both.

"Hell yeah, I'm game," Merlin told Alan.

CHAPTER 4

Hopix was looking Alan all over, making sure he was alright. "You sure you shook the entire spell off that the dark mage hit you with?" She was asking, looking even harder at his arm, hand, and shoulder.

Alan leaned down to where she was bent, looking at his legs and running her hands up and down then. 'Damn!' Alan thought, 'her touch is about to drive me nuts!' Grabbing both her hands sent a shock through both of them as Alan pulled her up to his level. "I have already checked myself, I am not seeing any of the energy left on or in me from the dark mage ok?"

Breathing a sigh of relief, Hopix looked straight into Alan's eyes a look of nothing but love there. "I have to make sure my husband," here she reached over and gently rubbed his crotch. "I have to make sure that you will be able to help me have children! My mom wants to be a grandmother as she has always wanted to be. I have to keep you healthy my love." Hopix demurely said.

Alan was on pins and needles Hopix's touch on his crotch had damned near made him pass out! What in the hell was going on? Alan looked over at Merlin, who was nodding his head with a huge grin.

Alan was sure now more than he had before, there must be something extremely special about a marriage between a human and a Fairixie. If her extra loving touch just now was any indication, he was in for a hell of a ride that was for sure.

Alan could hardly move after she let go with a little giggle, then he made his self-move; they had to end this and soon! Hopix was going to drive him crazy at this rate as he was sure he was her. Taking a deep breath Alan nodded to both of them then they all flashed out. A few miles away they appeared near a waterfall, the place was beautiful or was it? Alan concentrated the place changed to a smog filled, polluted water, twisted and dying tree area.

"So, you have come to face one of the strongest. I relish it there are so few to destroy now that bring true pleasure, come!" A rolling voice came from the dark water. Then a creature that seemed to be made of the filth of the place rose up from the muck.

Alan made a halfhearted fireball that was extinguished in a second. Suddenly the creature rose higher then fell upon Alan effectively covering him. Under the grime and muck Alan could see that this one was trying the same that the smoke creature. Alan first sent a freezing spell but saw it was ineffective, he thought. Suddenly an idea hit him as Alan began to alternate his spells cold, water, heat, and electricity.

At first, nothing happened, then there was a roaring scream then the entire creature started to tremble. Finally, a huge hole opened in front of Alan that was rapidly moving away from the hole he'd made. Screaming the creature reached out, touched the polluted water and was whole again. Screaming again, it started to wrap around Alan's shield. Alan just nodded and concentrated as he and the creature arose from the ground.

They were high above the planet within moments, "I was wondering if the vile pool was keeping you alive; now we will see!" Alan smiled as the creature turned and was at a loss as to where they were. Alan again hit it with the four spells in succession. This time the muck started to dry and harden; with a last scream Alan pushed out and the creature exploded off him.

Appearing next to Merlin and Hopix, Alan told them, "I suggest we move, what's left of it is coming this way at a high speed." Both of them nodded then they were standing a ways off, within moments, it appeared to be raining mud. "Well, that leaves three. What say we..." Suddenly there was a massive wave of water moving toward them. Alan sighed they never learned did they?

Alan set up a freezing barrier, but he felt it wouldn't last, the worse thing was these last four had used up quite a bit of his power. Alan looked at Merlin shaking his head, letting the man know he was a little used up. Merlin nodded back, opened his senses, and gave Alan as much power as possible. Alan was surprised that Merlin had as much power as he did.

Alan recharged, watched as Merlin smiled then promptly passed out. A slight wicked smile crossed his face as Alan suddenly increased the shield and started to walk toward the dark mage controlling this.

"It is of no matter Alan Glanto! I have felt your power falter, I know of your stored reserves they should be almost exhausted by now." Alan heard a voice thundering at him.

Alan smiled he had a little surprise for this ass! Still advancing, Alan suddenly increased the freezing effect hearing the dark mage scream as he tried to overcome Alan's attack. "Now you die!" Alan yelled at the mage.

"No! Your power was exhausted you had nothing Noooooooooooooo!!" with a final scream the dark mage was silent. Alan reached out not feeling that much from it; looking around the shield, Alan saw the water mage was frozen solid. Alan took a rock shattering the column of ice.

Grabbing Hopix and the unconscious Merlin, Alan thought of the sanctuary. Three sets of eyes had watched this last battle of Alan. They too had thought that Alan was finished then he suddenly had an abundance of power. The three strongest mages on the planet were more curious than much else. The champion was half tempted to kill the last two dark mages so he and Alan could finally have the battle he had been waiting a thousand years for. Shaking his head even though he had to follow the rules of the dark council. Oh well, the champion thought as he flashed out.

The last two dark mages knew that Alan was coming for them; next, their dark partner wasn't that far below either of them. They were going to have to set a trap it was the only way either of them were going to survive. They both agreed and left to set everything up to kill Alan Glanto long before he did them, hopefully.

Fools! The champion thought as he watched the last two flash out then the champion smiled. They were playing right into Alan's hands the way the champion had seen him do things; those two should be dead in a couple of days. Well, he thought with a sickening look of delight on his face we can hope can't we?

Alan, Hopix, and an unconscious Merlin appeared at the front of the sanctuary. Several Lobrits appeared, helping to carry Merlin inside. It's a good thing, Alan thought, as all the energy Merlin had given him was suddenly gone. Alan collapsed against the open doorway, unable to go another step. Hopix had gone ahead and turned to tell Alan something when she saw he wasn't with her.

Running back to the entrance, she found Alan trying to move further inside the entrance way. "Alan, my love, what's wrong?" A worried Hopix asked.

"The energy wasn't mine I was only borrowing it; once what I had to do was finished, it went back to its owner. I am not a dark mage I do not take and keep energy that isn't mine." Alan gasped out as he tried to move another two steps. He really didn't want the door open, putting the Lobrits in danger.

Hopix started to yell as several more Lobrits came up the corridor and helped Alan to move further inside. Sighing Alan was glad as he watched the door close. These people weren't the greatest but deserved a chance as everyone did. They barely got Alan in his cot when his eyes started to close.

"Thank you, Merlin that was dangerous. I am far

higher than you; my body could have taken more than it did." Alan told a now awake though slightly weak Merlin.

"I know my boy its ok, as I told you before, I have more tricks than you know. Now sleep we have a busy few days coming up." Here Merlin looked at a worried Hopix, "both of us." Alan nodded then surrendered to the darkness that had been creeping up on him.

Merlin motioned for Hopix to join him a moment. "Yes," she asked when she caught up to him at the back of the sanctuary.

"My dear I have a warning," here Merlin reached into a pocket and withdrew a cube not unlike the two that Hopix and Alan had.

The cube flashed momentarily, and then a circle of light appeared before Hopix. "Hello my dear," Came the voice of Queen Glimmer. "I have watched all that I could. Hopix you have to tell him, you know the danger if you don't. You may be afraid that he will leave you now, but if you wait it will be a disaster. Are you that anxious to die? After all that your mother went through saving the both of you, you are going to let this one secret kill the both of you?"

"I... I can't, not yet, it would be too big of a distraction to him. I am afraid that it would get him killed." Hopix stated as tears began to fall from her eyes.

The queen's face softened as she looked at Merlin the first good look she'd had of him in a very long time. "I had thought the same thing though it turned out to be a bigger push in Merlin's case. He tried to free all of the enslaved people. Then our world fell betrayed. Hopix tell him or you and many others will die. Your brother is still waiting to get married 'til he knows you are safe."

"I know my queen I will try but not 'til this is over, if it would help Alan I would tell him. I won't here 'til I feel this." A tearful Hopix replied.

"Alright my dear but there is far more than just you and Alan to consider. My love I have waited for you for so long you would be proud of you daughter Glimix she was so brave when Alan was rescuing our world I was so terrified. I had thought of using Glimix to hide in to protect the spirit of our people, and then I thought of Hopix." Glimmer was telling Merlin.

Merlin had tears in his eyes he hadn't seen Glimmer in so long. The bond was just as strong, but they were so far apart it hurt in a way Merlin had never felt. "It was the best choice that you could make my love I am glad that Alan saved you and the people, so glad. I owe this man far more than I can ever repay, though I'll try."

Hopix also had tears in her eyes everything might end in the next few days. It was all up to Alan as it had always been. She just hoped that Alan took the news better than she thought he might. Taking a sigh she shrugged; Alan had reacted far differently than she thought he would quite a few times.

Merlin shook his head at something Glimmer said. 'Yes,' he thought "Glimmer was a hell of a lot better judge of a person than almost anyone he knew was. Yes," he thought again, 'it just might work!'

Merlin had a plan, a plan that his Glimmer had

given him. Looking at Hopix he knew it was dangerous, Hopix's temper was almost legendary. Merlin smiled when he remembered the first time Glimmer had lost her temper at him, damn but that hadn't been a very good day that was for sure.

Sighing, first Alan had to defeat the last three. Merlin knew that the last two plain mages would be no problem but this champion was another matter altogether. There had to be something that he could do to help Alan. Snapping his fingers Merlin concentrated and created a small ball of light. Smiling he concentrated again and it vanished. 'There,' he thought, 'that might help, a little watch dog.'

Alan rolled over his head pounding, what the hell was going on? He didn't think he'd used that much energy as he thought back over all of the last battle. So that was why the water dark mage had been so confident! He'd been trying to drain Alan while he'd been attacking, basically using all of Alan's power he'd absorbed against Alan. Damn it! No wonder he'd been so weak afterward, unlike when Merlin gave him his power, the dark mage had actually used up all he took.

Another thing I really need to watch out for, Alan thought as the room stopped spinning. Opening his eyes, Alan looked around the room, huh, this was a first; he was actually alone. Thinking of Hopix a moment, his member got uncomfortably hard. Sighing, Alan thought, I'm going to die from just the want of her, long before the dark mages finish me.

Getting up Alan thought he ought to talk to Merlin about the energy draining spells. Looking all over the sanctuary, Alan started to get a little worried when he didn't see either in to protect the spirit of our people, and then I thought of Hopix." Glimmer was telling Merlin.

Merlin had tears in his eyes he hadn't seen Glimmer in so long. The bond was just as strong, but they were so far apart it hurt in a way Merlin had never felt. "It was the best choice that you could make my love I am glad that Alan saved you and the people, so glad. I owe this man far more than I can ever repay, though I'll try."

Hopix also had tears in her eyes; everything might end in the next few days. It was all up to Alan as it had always been. She just hoped that Alan took the news better than she thought he might. Taking a sigh she shrugged, Alan had reacted far differently than she thought he would quite a few times.

Merlin shook his head at something Glimmer said. "Yes," he thought "Glimmer was a hell of a lot better judge of a person than almost anyone he knew was. Yes," he thought again, "it just might work!"

Merlin had a plan, a plan that his Glimmer had given him. Looking at Hopix he knew it was dangerous, Hopix's temper was almost legendary. Merlin smiled when he remembered the first time Glimmer had lost her temper at him, damn but that hadn't been a very good day that was for sure.

Sighing, first Alan had to defeat the last three. Merlin knew that the last two plain mages would be no problem but this champion was another matter altogether. There had to be something that he could do to help Alan. Snapping his fingers Merlin concentrated and created a small ball of light.

Smiling he concentrated again and it vanished. 'There,' he thought, 'that might help, a little watch dog.'

Alan rolled over, his head pounding, what the hell was going on? He didn't think he'd used that much energy as he thought back over all of the last battle. So, that was why the water dark mage had been so confident! He'd been trying to drain Alan while he'd been attacking, basically using all of Alan's power he'd absorbed against Alan. Damn it! No wonder he'd been so weak afterward, unlike when Merlin gave him his power the dark mage had actually used up all he took.

Another thing I really need to watch out for, Alan thought as the room stopped spinning. Opening his eyes Alan looked around the room, huh, this was a first; he was actually alone. Thinking of Hopix a moment his member got uncomfortably hard. Sighing, Alan thought, I'm going to die from just the want of her, long before the dark mages finish me.

Getting up Alan thought he ought to talk to Merlin about the energy draining spells. Looking all over the sanctuary Alan started to get a little worried when he didn't see either

Merlin or Hopix. Walking back in Alan decided to eat before he did another thing. The main problem there was he couldn't eat what the people here did. He'd already had severe cramps from just a taste of the local food on another planet, shaking his head he wasn't really ready for that again.

Alan waved his hand and a few dishes he'd had at the diner appeared before him. The food piping hot, his mouth started to water, hell yeah!

He thought, 'that's more like it!' An hour later, still no Hopix or Merlin; Alan really started to get worried, reaching out he soon felt both of them not far from the sanctuary.

Flashing out, Alan appeared next to Merlin, and then his mouth dropped open. What in the hell was going on? Hopix was held suspended in the air in a spread eagle position, a look of fear on her face 'til she saw Alan.

"Merlin! What in the hell is going on? I sleep for a few hours and this happens? Talk old MAN!" Alan Roughly grabbed the front of Merlin's shirt.

Merlin's face was hurt as he tried to speak. "We had stepped out to get some air I didn't think they'd attack; they captured both us an hour ago. I cannot move from this spot, as I am afraid you are also stuck."

Alan scoffed at Merlin and almost ripped the man from where he's been stationary. Stepping up Alan had ripped over half of what was holding Hopix loose when a dark mage appeared.

"Uh, uh, uh keep it up and she dies, bastard! You might have defeated the others somewhat easily but that won't happen here." Alan lunged forward, freezing when Hopix screamed. "Sweet isn't she? Her screams will fuel my hatred for the human race for centuries. Now then try to save her, and she dies, move, and she dies. Be a good little boy, and stay right there as we eat your soul and power."

Another dark mage appeared, looking like a twisted, long-legged bird shape. Alan had been examining everything; suddenly, a smile lit up his face. "So you want me to stand still, ok, hit me if you can!" Alan growled as his face twisted into a mask of rage.

The second dark mage faltered a moment; Alan smiled more as the dark mage was suddenly a huge ball of flame. The first dark mage looked back at the second causing Alan to smile more. Waving his hand across the sight of Hopix in front of him, Alan felt her fade and reappear within his shield behind him.

"I knew as soon as I saw you that you would take every advantage you could. You have a lot of power and have more brains than the others. Well, you have a little more; here, I thought you had been watching me all this time. I am no simple fool as you thought I was. You are the last of an accursed blight upon this planet, it has been a while, but at last, this planet will be free!" Alan shouted as he threw several attacks at the dark mage at the same time.

Diving and twisting, the dark mage wasn't even aware when Alan appeared directly behind him. "You are dead! I have much more power than you!"

The dark mage was shocked when the dust and smoke cleared, and Alan was gone! Reaching out the dark mage felt nothing of the man, no wait what!? Turning the Dark mage saw Alan behind him, but how he'd felt nothing! "You were just out classed," Alan said as he made several slashing, flattening, and punching motions. Several cuts appeared, the dark mage was buffeted, and he was suddenly flying backwards all the breath knocked out of him. Appearing above the bleeding gasping mage Alan growled, " good bye you son of a bitch!"

The dark mage screamed as he caught fire, and

was suddenly flattened to a pulp. A clapping behind him made Alan whirl firing with all his rage. The champion's eyes grew large as he increased his shields. What in the hell? It wasn't enough as the bolts quickly ate through his shields smashing into his left arm. His own rage building the champion pointed his right hand at Alan.

"Just for that, you little bitch!" The champion growled out, "I'm going to kill you as slowly as I can!"

"Yeah right! You and what army, you pathetic little ass! Have fun healing; there is none higher than us here. Though you could beg the dark council, I'm sure they'd love to help you. Oh yeah, that's right they aren't allowed! Go away little boy!"

The champion growled again then was gone, though Alan knew he wouldn't get that far with his injury. Turning Alan tenderly picked up Hopix, and nodded to Merlin and flashed back to the sanctuary. Alan was just starting to take her into the sanctuary when her eyes briefly opened, "I'm sorry, my love, I'm sorry I haven't told you who I am. Who my family is, I was so afraid that I would lose you. I love you more than life itself. My mother you have met before, my father, you also know."

Hopix's skin started to glow, again Alan could only stare. What was going on with her? This was much like on the other Fairixie world when she confessed that she wasn't what she appeared to be. "What are you trying to tell me?" Alan asked her.

"I have denied who I am for so long out of the guilt I have felt. It was a mage I trained that betrayed and enslaved my home. I never allowed myself to grow close to anyone 'til I met you. Please forgive me, my love." Here Hopix's body started to levitate out of Alan's arms.

Turning to look at Merlin the old man was smiling tears falling from his eyes. "Merlin? What in the hell is going on here?" Merlin only shook his head and motioned toward Hopix.

"Again, my love," Hopix's voice stated as it grew louder. "I am sorry I hid it from you, I was so afraid of losing you, even as I am right now." Her eyes flashing as the glow around her radiated brighter from her.

Suddenly the light council appeared, Hopix's friend Nealiex standing at the front with a proud look on her face as tears were streaming down her face. Then the cube in Merlin's hand flashed and a vision of the queen appeared next to Nealiex, tears also in her eyes. "Finally," Alan heard her say.

Floating to an almost standing position, a strange authoritative voice issued from Hopix's mouth. "For centuries I have denied who I truly am, what I am. As of today I can no longer do this." Here she looked at Alan. "I wish to accept Alan Glanto's union promise if he still wishes to after this. Before all assembled, before my family and friends, I now declare myself as Hopimer, First Princess of the Fairixie home world; next in line for the throne." Here she looked at Alan, "I know you have to decide you have a day, then either way the waiting ends.

Hopix now Hopimer lowered her voice as she spoke to Alan, "I love you with all that I am my love. I'll understand if you reject me." With that all but Merlin vanished.

Alan stood there in shock what in the hell had just happened? Where in the hell had everyone gone, especially Hopix? "Alright talk old man. What in the fuck is going on? Why didn't you give me a hint or something?!!"

Sighing Merlin sat, "I couldn't Alan it is their law, they have to declare and relate all things about them their selves. I, especially as an outsider could say nothing, even if she is my daughter."

Pissed as hell Alan growled about to punch Merlin in the face but struck the wall instead. "What the fuck! Does everyone think that I am a child they have to spare the feelings of? Give me a break!"

"Just tell me one thing Alan. Do you love my daughter?" Merlin asked praying that the answer he got was the right one.

"Of course I love her! Christ what in the hell is up with you people! I'm not a damn machine that can just turn it off and on!" Alan shouted still pissed.

"Look Alan it has..." Merlin started.

"NO! You look old man! I have an asshole to kill, so that these people no longer live in fear. If I die then problem solved, we aren't bonded yet so she'll survive. If I live? Then I come back here and I kick the shit out of you! Agreed?" Alan said his eyes flashing the anger he felt.

Merlin smiled so Alan wasn't against his daughter yet, good they needed to build on that. "You might find that harder than you think but you can try young man."

"HA!" Alan shouted back over his shoulder as he stormed out of the sanctuary.

The champion smiled as he looked at the clone

that Alan had defeated with ease. Turning toward the sanctuary he felt the ultra-high power spike. Damn he thought it felt like that bitch of Alan's. Appearing outside the sanctuary the champion's mouth dropped open as he watched everything. Damn it! She was no longer Hopix! Under the agreement, she was free, then he smiled, good this ought to screw Alan up enough to make him an easier target.

The champion waited a while, then saw an extremely angry Alan leave the sanctuary. Ah! Good now to declare his right to start the battle now.

Appearing in front of Alan far from the Sanctuary, the champion smiled. "I think it's time to end this, or are you too tired?"

"You really don't want to do this right now," Alan warned the man.

"Oh, but I do, you ass wipe, shall we?" The champion sneered as he started to power up.

"Fine, you that eager to die so be it!" Alan said as the champion mockingly nodded at Alan.

Alan contacted Merlin letting him know he was about to start the last battle. He needed to get all the Lobrits to safety UNDER their cities. Alan told the man that he knew he now had the power, he needed to hurry this was going to be extremely messy.

At first they just threw a few bolts at each other, feeling each other out. Satisfied the champion suddenly started to fire with increasing power at Alan. Several bolts missed as Alan thought they might. Flashing out and behind the champion at the last second the man was shocked as his own attacks hit his shields.

"Nice move ass wipe now then..." the champion started just as Alan let loose an extremely powerful bolt. The champion's mouth dropped open as he could feel its heightened power fueled by Alan's rage. Hitting his shields it sliced through, brushing the champion's left leg. Screaming he retaliated smashing Alan's shields with a myriad of attacks.

It seemed they were going for hours; the champion was a little frustrated. Everything he'd learned about Alan was doing no good he had to resort to something of desperation soon if this kept up. The champion could feel his power actually dwindle a bit. No he thought I have plenty Alan will fade long before I do.

Alan wasn't all that sure he could defeat this little piss ant as of yet, except for the first bolt. Alan had only been fighting the champion to a standstill. Though he'd used a hell of a lot of power Alan still had a huge reserve if he had to resort to it. As of yet, he thought he was still good though.

For another hour, they continued to fire at each other. Now four hours into the fight, they were both starting to pant a bit. The gash on the left leg of the champion still wouldn't close, though he'd sent abundant healing to it. There were a few bruises on both arms but nothing compared to the wound the white mage had given him.

Alan had small cuts across his face, chest, arms, and legs, and face was now bruised. Still Alan had only been fighting the champion to a stalemate. Damn it Alan though not sure I can keep this up all that much longer, this is as tiring as straight battling was.

It was four and a half hours into the fight when Alan made his first mistake, instead of avoiding a bolt from the champion, Alan took it full as it sliced across his shoulder. Laughing, the Champion had dropped his protection, as Alan fired through the pain catching the champion's left arm. Smiling Alan heard the man scream as the bolt burned the arm to a useless piece of meat.

The champion's eyes flashed as he started to send several bolts at Alan again, this time one actually got through, hitting his right leg. Sealing it as fast as he could Alan felt a little better, then felt his power falter a bit as he started to sink toward the ground. Looking over he could see that the champion was also sinking fast toward the remnants of the largest city. Shaking his head Alan thought I'll have to try and rebuild these. Hate that we destroyed the other two already.

Alan tried to reach out to find the champion. Alan was surprised when he felt that the champion was as weak as he was now. Maybe I've got a chance Alan thought if this goes on with us using our powers, we'll be into our life force before too long. Merlin appeared not long after they had both sunk toward the land. Shaking his head Merlin thought this was going on far too long for his tastes. There wasn't a whole lot he could do, he could help in small ways only energy or healing but no actual fighting.

Searching like Alan had taught him, he could feel the champion in front of him. Damn, the man was so weak compared to what he had been, when Merlin had gotten his ass handed to him by the man.

There Alan was! Holy crap! Alan was weaker than Merlin was! Hell Merlin was stronger than both of them right now. Flashing out near Alan, Merlin knew he had to stay as far away as he could. "Alan?" Merlin said before he rounded the corner behind Alan.

"I'm around the corner from you," Merlin heard Alan's whispering voice.

"Why are you here? You cannot interfere." Alan told the man.

"I know that Alan, but I can provide aid, he's on the other side of the city. I felt that your power was dropping as was his. As it is right now I have more power than both of you. Strange feeling knowing I am the most powerful mage on the planet right now." Looking at Alan, Merlin said, "I don't like it! Nope not at all." This of course, made Alan smile the old man was nothing if not honest.

Merlin started to add his own power to Alan's. Sighing he knew it wasn't a lot of help but at least his levels were high enough for Alan to use. Alan nodded making Merlin stop, the man was a little light headed. "Alright, try to get away from here at least a little way. That way I know you'll be ok."

Merlin swayed a little, then sat back a minute, nodding; he smiled and vanished. Well, Alan thought both of our powers are nearly exhausted. This rest won't really help though with what Merlin had loaned him, Alan might actually have a chance.

Merlin actually managed to get to a hill side that overlooked what was left of the city. Damn, he thought as he appeared and stumbled to the remnants of a smoldering tree. Taking the cube out of his pocket tears falling from his eyes he whispered, "I'm sorry my darling, I guess I did too much. I gave him almost everything; he deserves the chance to be with Hopimer." Crying harder, he kissed her image as he felt the last of his strength leave his body. "I did so wish to hold you one last time before I died; please forgive me my love." With that the darkness took him even as a scream erupted from the cube.

Recharged at least half way Alan started to make his way toward where he felt the champion. This has to end, Alan thought. Fifteen minutes later Alan slowed feeling the champion not far away.

"Hey ass wipe I know you're there, stick your head around the corner I'll make it quick that way this is done then I can rest and eat your soul," came the champion's voice.

"You know you talk too much," Alan said as he rolled out and fired at the champion in the other leg, dropping the man to the turf. Still rolling Alan was behind cover again when he felt his good arm bleeding. Damn it! Looking out, he saw what appeared to be something that looked a lot like glass. Shit!

Alan leaned out for a quick look seeing that the champion had crawled behind cover himself. Moving quickly, Alan moved as close as he could, ducking behind cover as the champion let loose a barrage of energy blasts. "Feeling better now, prick?" The champion yelled, "I saw you were bleeding; kind of stupid moving without checking the terrain."

Alan smirked, almost as stupid as taking on an enemy he knew little to nothing about. "You're a fine one to talk can't walk or use one arm, personally, I think you are about done!"

"Oh, I've got more than enough to kill you, besides after I take your power, I won't have to worry." The champion yelled back.

Alan was about to make a move when a round light orb appeared. Flashing a scene a moment Alan smiled, damn, why hadn't he thought of that? Alan could see the champion was huddled against the wall in front of him had he gone in, he might be dead now. Alan nodded to the orb, which winked out Alan started to climb the wall on the far side of it.

Looking down Alan saw that the champion was still waiting on him to make a frontal attack. Aiming Alan let loose with three bolts the last of the power that Merlin had given him. One caught the champion in the chest, another in his already injured arm. The third shot barely missed destroying everything between the champion's legs.

Alan listened to the screams of the champion as he climbed down and walked to what was left of the man. The man's eyes went wide when he saw Alan trying to power up. Alan waggled his finger at the man, knocking him out with a solid kick.

Barely standing, Alan yelled, "I call the light and dark councils. After they had both appeared in the dark council seething that their champion was unconscious, Alan spoke again. "I have defeated the dark council champion; I, therefore, call for a judgment."

"This fight was to the death!" The leader of the dark council spit out.

"No, as I remember you said when he killed me, you got us both. My part was if I win not a death, I need a judgment this pitiful creature can no longer fight. Therefore by the wagering the dark council made with me, they can no longer interfere in the affairs of earth. I and my life are also off limits, this includes any worlds that I have visited or am living on."

The leader of the light council was smiling from ear to ear. Yes, Alan had made that wager, and yes, he had won.

"I call for a judgment," the leader of the light council called. All of the members agreed that the champion could no longer fight.

Suddenly there was a groan from the creature/man, "Excuse me a moment, ' Alan said and kicked the champion again in the face, "Ok, he's out again." The entire dark council growled at Alan, and then all slowly started to agree the champion was finished.

"We need a ruling lived Reficul, or are you risking the rightful evoking of your true identities?" The leader of the light council smiled.

"No! We are all in agreement. All that was agreed to will be fulfilled know this, Alan Glanto, anywhere else you go we will be there. In this respect we will always be watching you!" The leader of the dark council stated. With that the dark council and their champion disappeared.

Alan nodded then took a step toward the sanctuary; that was the last thing he remembered for at least two days.

Hopix was smiling down at Alan, god he thought she was so beautiful. Alan loved her so much, but he was going to die, there was nothing that he could do. Crying he held her as close as he could, he knew there wasn't much time but he had to hold her a last time.

It was almost three days later when Alan opened his eyes, shaking his head he was in the cheap motel room. Where was Hopix? They said they needed a decision, hanging his head he nodded they had used him. Just like his wife had. Tears erupted from his eyes; I truly loved her now there was nothing left with her gone.

Reaching in his pocket the cube was even gone, so they had all lied to him. 'Well, ' Alan thought, 'that's about my life.' Alan walked out, might as well go eat. got to get a job, sighing Alan shut and locked the door.

On the bed's far side, a light erupted near the floor as did a voice. "Alan? My love, are you there? Mother, father I can feel him his energy is so low. I have to go to him, I don't care!" There was a titanic eruption of energy then a lightly green skin colored woman, six foot tall appeared out of a rift.

Bending down she could feel the cube, then she found it under the bed. Shaking her head Alan was so confused, why had the cube brought him back here? Then her mouth dropped open of course, home! The energy of the planet he was born on had the strongest healing energy.

Looking in the mirror, Hopimer smiled; this would become far easier with her absolute power. Waving her hand her appearance changed. Smiling she nodded; that ought to do, oh! She best wear clothes, she giggled. Walking out she followed the very low energy of Alan to a strange metal building, taking a deep breath she entered.

Alan had taken a seat at the back in a booth by

himself, as depressed as he was he hoped everyone left him alone. Looking up a beautiful six foot slender red head walked in the door. Damn Alan thought that is one gorgeous woman.

Then the amazing happened she came to his table! "May I sit with you?" she asked with the sweetest voice that he'd heard since Hopix's. Looking harder at the woman, damn if she didn't look a lot like Hopix.

"Are you alright sir," she asked.

"No not really," Alan replied. "I lost the most beautiful woman I have ever met. I guess she was taken from me.

The job I had, my bosses lied to me, and apparently everything I did for them was for nothing. I woke up in my hotel room alone without my ride I got from some good friends, well I thought they were. So no I am not alright, sorry, I'm not good company."

"Oh my god! I am so sorry Alan," the woman said, causing Alan's head to snap up and then he was staring at her.

"How do you know my name?" A stunned Alan asked.

"Why wouldn't I know my future husband's name?" The woman said as she giggled a bit.

"Ho ... Hopix?" Alan barely managed to get out. When she only smiled and nodded Alan could only stare at her. "But you're human looking, they can all see you!"

"Thanks to you I have almost all my full power. You disappeared right after you fell near the Lobrit's city. We all became frantic searching for you.

Apparently the Trembly's felt you would die if you didn't heal on earth. I finally felt you a few minutes ago. Please, Alan can we go home? You still have to declare your decision." Hopimer explained. "Oh, and Alan my name is Hopimer now, I wear it as the next in line for the throne."

Alan nodded as they got up and left. Alan stopped and kissed Hopimer deeply and passionately, causing her to almost pass out. Hopimer handed Alan his cube as the realization settled in. Alan smiled wider; ducking into a nearby alley, there was a sudden flash of light, then nothing.

Five years later, Alan was chasing the twins Donax and Glamix. Alan was far happier than he'd been in a very long time. The simple fact that Hopimer conceived their wedding night was nothing compared to the completion of their bond. Everything was hundreds of times better; his vision, his feelings, and did he mention the sex?

Hopimer watched the three loves of her life. Though she wasn't queen yet she sighed, there were still official things she had to do. She missed going out to different places. Suddenly a thought hit here; grabbing both of their seldom used cubes Hopimer walked up to the twins and Alan.

"I was thinking we need to take a trip!" She told all three of them.

"Sure hon; anywhere in particular?" Alan asked as she grabbed Alan's and the children's hands.

"I was thinking the Trembly's world," Leaning over Hopimer kissed Alan then started to whisper in his ear.

Alan got wide eyed, smiled, and whispered,

"You are?" Hopimer nodded as she touched her stomach, and they all vanished.

The End

OTHER BOOKS BY THE AUTHOR

Karmic Love

Undercover

Eternal Love

Undying Lust

The Good Taste

Offence and Justice

A Model for Murder

Lethal Legacy

Lethal Legacy 2

Paranormal Club

Enchanted Souls

Beginners of Nowhere

Wildflower

Mystic Agent

Dark Angel

Lonesome Moonlight

The Eerie Egg

A Romantic Crime .

Passionate Alien

Dragon Knight

The Critical Case

In the Shadow

Mental Asylum

Athena

Candy Spy

Hidden Veil

www.ingramcontent.com/pod-product-compliance
Lightning Source LLC
Chambersburg PA
CBHW071139180726
48291CB00007B/2258